STILL THE ONE

FAMILY STONE #4 JACK

LISA HUGHEY

STILL THE ONE

by
Lisa Hughey

February 2014

Lisa Hughey

Ebook ISBN: 978-0-9840428-9-0

Print ISBN: 978-0-9991951-6-1

Cover Artwork – © 2018 L.J. Anderson of Mayhem Cover Creations

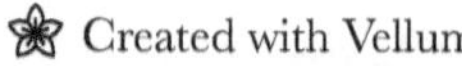 Created with Vellum

"I'll be in DC in six hours." Jackson Stone, Junior, slammed down the receiver on his office landline and cursed silently.

Nothing like the past coming back to bite you in the ass.

He rubbed his tired eyes and huffed out a breath. He had twenty things on his plate but two took precedence over everything else.

First, Jack called Shane and had him get the Bombardier Challenger 604 jet ready for a trip to DC. "I'll be at the Monterey Regional Airport in two hours." *One down.*

Second, he could make inroads with his brother Connor. Con continued to hold back and no matter what Jack said, he knew that his younger brother was still trying to make up for his hellish teenage years.

"Connor!" Jack yelled through the doorway of his office and waited for his brother to get from his office to Jack's.

He didn't know why Connor couldn't just get over it and focus on now. That was how Jack handled life. The past was the past. But Jack was determined to get Connor comfortably in the family fold. This was the perfect opportunity to show Con he had complete trust in him.

At least this would solve one of his family problems. He'd have Connor run the office at Global Humanitarian Relief and Stone Consulting for the few days he'd be gone. Jack's stomach cramped. Shit, he did not want to make this trip.

If only he didn't have to see Bliss again.

Clearly, he needed to take his own advice. The past was in the past.

The thought of having to interact with her, to work with her, sent a dagger through his heart. He wasn't sure whether the proximity would make him want to kiss her or kill her.

But he'd do neither. Jack had to hold on to his anger, keep it brewing and keep it high, because thirteen years ago when she'd told him they were over, she'd gutted him. He couldn't go back to that dark, lost place again.

He'd never told a soul how much her rejection had hurt him.

Instead, he'd arrived at the Great Lakes Naval Training Center and thrown himself into being the best damn recruit and graduate of Basic the U.S. Navy had ever seen.

The loss of Bliss, and what they had, took years to get over. And if there were any way that he could have avoided this request, demand really, to work with her and her agency, he would have sold his soul to do it.

Anger was the only way he'd get through this assignment with his heart unscathed. He'd long since stopped thinking about her every day but there was no question that she was the measure of how he had judged every single woman he'd dated since. And after how long it had taken to get over her, he'd been determined never to let another woman have that kind of power over him again. And he'd succeeded.

He had casual relationships with nice, hot women who never touched any part of him except his dick.

Jack rubbed his hand over his face. He needed to focus on his assignment and not Bliss.

Con stomped into Jack's office. "What the hell is your deal?"

"I need you," Jack said and watched unexpected happiness roll over Con's face.

"What for?"

"Close the door for a sec."

Con shut the door and raised his blond eyebrows. He stood in front of Jack's desk, military stiff, feet apart, hands clasped behind his back in parade rest.

"At ease, soldier." Jack chuckled. "While I love the fact that you consider me like your commanding Lord and Master—"

Con snorted.

"You're out of the Army now," Jack continued. "There's no need for military protocol in the office."

"I'm comfortable with it," he said simply.

Jack's moment of amusement was gone, replaced by a somber frown. "Okay. I have to be out of the office for a few days. Unfortunately." He shifted in his massive desk chair and his mouth flattened into a grimace as he thought about why he needed Con.

They had a little over a week to find a missing witness. The only living proof that José Fernandez was a dirty fucking bastard. On the surface, Fernandez looked totally clean. He was the poster boy for promoting safe conditions for workers and making the lives of the working poor better. He'd made his career by protesting the treatment of the immigrant and migrant communities in regards to law enforcement, after the police hadn't given enough priority to the unsolved abductions of four teenage Mexican immigrant girls eight years ago.

Fernandez had shined a spotlight on the inequities in treatment of crimes against the poor and in the process made a name for himself politically. Since that horrible tragedy—none of the girls were ever found—he had worked tirelessly to make things better and earned a reputation as a vocal champion of the poor. He'd parlayed that original protest into an eight year career culminating in his nomination for Deputy Secretary of Labor.

Congress seemed poised to approve his appointment without much fuss. The guy had almost unheard of bi-partisan support.

"So do you need intel for your trip?"

"No." Jack's frown got deeper. Bliss's agency was handling the intel. "That part is taken care of."

Jack stared off into the distance. Fuck him, he really didn't want to see her again. He rubbed a hand over his mouth and shook his head. He needed to get back to Con.

"Muscle?" Con asked with bemusement.

Another smile quirked Jack's mouth. "Pretty sure of yourself, aren't you?"

Con shrugged.

"It's a Stone Consulting job," Jack clarified. "Classified."

Recently new evidence had been uncovered that indicated José Fernandez may have actually had a hand in the abduction of the girls and what happened to them.

They had found one living survivor. She'd been imprisoned in a house not even ten miles from where she'd been abducted eight years ago. Somehow, she'd escaped and gotten from rural California farm country to Washington DC. But Jack was sketchy on the details regarding how she got from one end of the country to the other.

Adams-Larsen International and Associates, Bliss's agency, had given Maria Torres new papers, a new place to live, and money to hide until authorities could gather additional evidence and Fernandez could be revealed as a corrupt fake and guilty man before the Senate voted on his confirmation. However, law enforcement needed all their ducks in a row before they went after Fernandez. And the execution of revealing the details had to be handled carefully. So the plan had been to keep her sequestered and safe until the time was right. Only Maria had taken her new documents, all the money, and disappeared. Again.

They had one week to find her before the confirmation hearing.

Right now all they had was Maria's deposition testimony, and the depositions of the people who'd helped hide her once she escaped. Only a handful of people knew that Maria Torres was alive and her accusation that José Fernandez had been behind her abduction and imprisonment.

But without Maria, they were dead in the water. No body, no person, no proof. Jack wondered what the hell she'd been thinking when she ran.

Had Fernandez somehow gotten wind that not only had she escaped but that she'd told someone about her ordeal? As far as they knew, she was the only person who could identify Fernandez as being involved in the eight-year-old case.

They needed to find her before Fernandez did.

While Jack and Bliss were looking for Maria, Jack would have Con working another angle. Jack wanted Connor to dig into Fernandez's background. "I really need your help on a separate job." Jack stared out the reflective glass window, the view of the Monterey Bay obscured by lingering morning fog. Wisps of clouds drifted lazily in the gray sky. He loved being back home. Loved living near the ocean again. Loved that he was making a go of the company with his siblings.

When Connor just waited patiently, Jack finally said, "You can get so quiet it's freaky. How are we even related?"

And shit, as soon as it came out of his mouth he realized his mistake. Con stiffened but didn't say a word. Hopefully his faith Connor's computer abilities would make up for Jack putting his foot in his mouth again.

"Can you run an intensive background check on José Fernandez?"

"Sure." Connor said, "Am I looking for anything specific?"

"I don't know." Jack rubbed his finger along his scarred eyebrow. If there was something there, any other hint of Fernandez's complicity in the old crime or even a newer one, Con would find it. They could use whatever Con could dig up in case they couldn't find Maria before the confirmation hearing.

The scandal was going to be crazy.

"I need anything and everything you can find on the guy. There's got to be something there, even if no one has found it yet. I don't want to influence your search, so I'm keeping it vague."

Jack had given him a puzzle and he knew Con's interest was piqued. "You got it. Anything else?"

It was extremely important that they didn't tip Fernandez off. "Don't tell anyone what you're working on."

Con shrugged as if that wouldn't be a problem.

"Stay here a sec." Jack pressed the intercom on his phone and called his assistant, Ava Sanchez. "Ava, my office now."

Finding Maria Torres would be the ultimate coup, for many reasons. But the best of all would be easing Ava's guilt. Ava would be over the moon to find out that her best friend from high school wasn't dead. Ava was more than his employee, she was like a little sister, and Jack was thrilled that he would have a hand in helping Ava put the guilt behind her. He couldn't wait to see the reunion of Ava and Maria.

Reunion. Ugh. That reminded him of what he'd have to do in order to make that reunion happen. He'd have to have a reluctant reunion of his own.

If only he didn't have to see Bliss again.

CHAPTER 2

Bliss Lee rubbed her damp palms over her navy blue, Federally-approved pantsuit, and forced herself not to pace the elegantly appointed CEO's office of Adams-Larson International and Associates, lovingly and humorously dubbed ALIAS by the employees. She was the 'Associates' part of the agency. Which was fine by her. She didn't want the responsibility of running the whole shebang. She'd rather concentrate on their special clients.

"Relax," Jillian Larson, her boss, friend, and co-chairman of Adams-Larsen directed and threw up hands. "He's just a guy."

But Jack Stone wasn't just a guy. He was *The Guy*. The one who got away, even though she'd initiated their break-up. The one who, despite her attempts to find another guy, ruined her for every other man she'd ever been intimate with. Except that had been their problem. Jack Stone didn't really know how to be intimate.

Sex, yes. Emotional intimacy, no.

He'd been excellent at the sex part. But he'd never bared his private self to her. Although she'd had her own issues with being completely honest, she'd tried as much as she could. Her lack of honesty was more omission than lying. But her awkward half-attempts and Jack's inability had been too much strain for their young relationship. And once he'd joined the Navy, she'd been done.

Unfortunately, Bliss had never found another bond close to what she'd had with Jack, flaws and all. Even her ex-husband couldn't measure up to Jack Stone. And after a long two years of trying to make their marriage work, they had, less than amicably, decided to end it. Her ex-husband had accused her of hiding things. And she had been. Most of all she'd been hiding the fact that she was still in love with a man she'd kicked out years earlier.

Bliss's throat tightened. "Keep telling me that."

Jillian raised one exquisitely-groomed blond eyebrow and smirked. "Gladly." Her friend was perfectly put together in her signature pencil skirt in black and a fitted black jacket with a flirty peplum accent.

Bliss couldn't pull off that outfit in a million years. Jill looked sophisticated, sexy, and in charge. Bliss stuck to borderline masculine suits and darted white or blue broadcloth shirts.

The intercom crackled. "Your appointment has arrived," Marissa said pleasantly through the communication system.

Bliss's heart boomed in her chest, furious and nearly out-of-control.

Jill's hand wrapped around Bliss's wrist tightly, grounding her, reining her in. Bliss took a deep breath, gathered her scattered composure, and nodded. "Ready."

"Show him in," Jillian said calmly to Marissa.

The perfunctory knock was quick and then the door

swung open. Bliss forced herself to turn, braced for the impact of seeing Jack Stone again.

Jack strode into the office like he owned it. Dressed in khaki cargo pants and a black t-shirt, the cotton strained across his forty-six inch chest, his huge biceps tested the hem of his short sleeves. He had a canvas duffel slung over his shoulder and a multi-dial watch strapped to his solid, thick wrist.

He didn't falter when his gaze connected with hers, but she was pretty sure his shoulders tightened almost imperceptibly. They locked gazes, his ever-changing hazel eyes appeared almost pure green today and mesmerized her with their intensity.

The shock of his penetrating regard held her immobile. She damned her extreme visceral reaction as stunning emotions and images from years ago waterfalled through her brain; Joy, Jack laughing as he picked her up and swung her around like she was a kid; Love, Jack lying in bed, sheets tangled around his legs, his large chest bare, arm propped behind his head, eager smile on his face, as he waited impatiently for her to join him; Lust, Jack with water droplets running down his body and disappearing into the wrap of his towel, the bulge of his erection a sign of his passion; Pain, Jack's stunned expression when she told him goodbye; and finally despair, the stark, unrelenting ache that gripped her for weeks and months after he'd left.

Each image and the emotion behind the remembrance pierced her heart, until she was sure she must be bleeding out onto Jill's intricately woven, twenty-thousand-dollar Persian carpet.

Jack stopped in front of Jillian, dropped his duffel to the floor, and held out his solid, wide palm. "Jack Stone." His hands were big and scarred and tough, just like the rest of him. Those hands had caressed every inch of her body and brought her to heights of ecstasy that she hadn't climbed since he'd left.

He looked good. Damn him. Better than good, great. He had some new lines around his eyes, and his hair was a little longer. His face had matured, the softness of the young adult he'd been was now honed to a sharpness that only ramped up his attractiveness. A thin strip of hair was missing from his right eyebrow, a white scar creased the arch, and her heart stopped as she recognized that the missing strip was likely from a bullet graze.

He'd almost had his head blown off.

She swallowed down the fear that mushroomed through her. Based on the faded whiteness of the scar, the damage had happened a long time ago.

He'd filled out since she'd last seen him, and he'd already been big to begin with. His physical size had been comforting and engendered a feeling of safety and security for a girl who'd had far too much upheaval and violence in her early life.

Not that Jack knew anything about that, of course. She'd never told him about her childhood. She wasn't supposed to tell anyone. Ever.

Jillian introduced herself, then said, "This is my associate, Bliss Lee."

Jack nodded briefly at Bliss, but didn't offer his hand. Instead he propped his hand on his waist. "We've met."

We've met? *We've met?* That's it? That was how he was going to acknowledge their history to her boss? "Jack," she said firmly, refusing to let him see the pain his presence and his casual dismissal of their past relationship brought. She couldn't bring herself to say it was nice to see him.

Jack kept his focus on Jillian and barely acknowledged Bliss's presence. "Let's get down to business."

"Would you like a cup of tea or coffee?" Jillian offered politely.

Bliss was still stuck in the same spot, rooted to the floor. He'd spoken of the most influential and impactful relationship of her life as if it were a random, accidental encounter in a crowded cafeteria. *We've met?*   ·

"What I'd like, is to find Maria Torres." His abrupt shift from observing niceties to cold, hard soldier was just what she needed.

That jolted Bliss and she realized it was time to take over this meeting. Enough of the old memories and the old Bliss. She wasn't the same girl she'd been when they'd ended and it was time Jack Stone figured that out.

"Agreed." Bliss gestured to the brocade wing chair in the grouped seating off to the side of Jillian's desk. "Have a seat."

She marched over to the other wing chair and sat down as elegantly as possible. She picked up the dossier that held all the information they had about Maria Torres. Everything that Bliss had used to relocate her to a safe house where she didn't have to worry about being found by José Fernandez. And yet Maria Torres had blown out of that safe house, and almost guaranteed safety, within hours of getting settled there.

Bliss hadn't ever lost a client this way and the fact that she hadn't realized that Maria intended to rabbit from the safe house—as soon as Bliss left—rankled. Maria hadn't given any indication that she was skittish or worried about her safety. Maria had listened and absorbed everything that they had told her. Promises to keep her safe. Assurances that

José Fernandez would not find her. A guard close by in town if she needed anything.

Maria had seemed to accept their reassurances. But then she'd left.

Bliss understood the fear. Better than most. But Maria was less safe wandering around the country without the protection of Adams-Larsen than she had been tucked in that little Iowa farm town, and Bliss still couldn't understand why Maria had felt the need to bolt. But Bliss had to put aside her ego and find Maria damn quick before José Fernandez did.

They knew that her prison guards would have learned of Maria's escape from her confinement in Salinas a few days ago. They visited once a week to drop off food and pick up garbage. Maria had left the moment they had departed her prison last week. But they would have been back this week and discovered that she was gone.

Adams-Larsen and the U.S. Marshals were confident that Fernandez was now looking for Maria based on a cryptic phone conversation between Fernandez and two unknown accomplices. Adams-Larsen was pretty sure that Fernandez had panicked and was trying to tie up loose ends.

They still had no proof, besides Maria's officially documented and audio-taped testimony, that Fernandez was guilty of kidnapping and false imprisonment. And they couldn't bring those facts to light until they had their only eyewitness in hand.

No court of law would convict or even allow the taped evidence without the actual witness live and in person. Or without some other authority to validate the credibility of the witness. Otherwise everything was just hearsay and could be thrown out of court and Adams-Larsen left themselves open to a slander charge.

As far as Fernandez's reputation, there might be a blip on the political meter, but without any proof, without Maria, they were screwed. He'd get off scot free.

José Fernandez was the scum of the earth and Bliss wanted to nail him to the wall and watch him bleed. Watch his life be crushed, just like he'd crushed Maria's spirit for the last eight years. Bastard.

"This is her last known location." Bliss pointed to the small farming town on the map as Jack seated himself in the delicate chair. His shoulders were nearly as broad as the chair back and his large frame dwarfed the feminine lines of the chair, causing a tingle deep inside at his sheer size and dominating presence. Until he opened his mouth.

"Iowa?" Jack frowned. "What the hell was she doing in Iowa?"

Bliss stiffened. She'd worked tirelessly to get Maria to a place where she'd be at ease and could try to reintegrate into the world. To a place where she would feel comfortable enough to actually have a life and not just hole up in a new, different prison.

"Are you an expert in witness relocation, Mr. Stone?" Jillian asked graciously, a pleasant and almost vacuous smile on her classically beautiful face. Thank God for Jill.

Jack was zipping through the contents of the file Bliss had handed him, absorbing information. Even while he responded and questioned the contents, he was assimilating. She'd forgotten about his innate ability to multi-task. Jack had a brilliant mind. Which had made his decision to go into the military and use his brawn an even odder choice to her. A more heartbreaking choice. He could have been anything. Done anything. And he'd chosen to put his life on the line. And while his intentions were honorable, Bliss had not been able to handle even the potential for any more violence and loss in her life.

But she couldn't tell Jack that. She hadn't told him that the thought of him in danger left her with nightmares. She'd started waking up in the middle of the night sweating, her fight or flight instinct triggered, her heart tripping like she'd been discovered. The nightmares had brought back all the fear and sadness she'd spent years trying to overcome.

He'd never even noticed that she'd been totally freaked out. Either that or he hadn't cared enough to ask what was wrong. After weeks of worry and stress, she'd realized that she wasn't going to be able to do it. To be able to live with the fact that Jack would be under constant threat of danger. Just the thought of him in peril brought too many of her own demons screaming to the forefront of her mind.

And he may have been shocked when she'd told him they were done. But he'd never tried, not once, to talk it out with her. He'd just packed up his stuff and left. She may have verbally ended their relationship but he'd physically ended it by walking away. By not fighting for them like he'd planned to fight for their country.

"No." He fingered the papers in the file. "But I would have thought you'd place her somewhere with at least a decent amount of Spanish speakers."

"Her English is better than her Spanish now," Bliss informed him. "She spent the last eight years alone with a television set that only received three English speaking channels. She hasn't spoken Spanish in a very long time."

Bliss hesitated. She hated to explain herself but since he was here and needed to work with them, needed to work with her...he needed a firmer grasp of the oddities of this situation.

Maria's placement was radically different from their usual 'special' clients. Normally the client came to them and wanted to disappear. They had already come to terms with the realities of taking on a new life to be safe. They knew if they followed the rules, they could escape the threat that plagued them.

Maria Torres was a completely unique case.

She'd been imprisoned below ground, in a dank basement, for eight years. Her only contact with the outside world had come from three television channels and the pigs who checked on her once a week. They shoved bags of food and clothing in through a small cat door and retrieved her garbage bags using a long metal trash grabber. She rarely even saw their faces.

At twenty-three, she'd basically been in isolation for one third of her lifetime.

The psychological impact of her imprisonment would likely take years of therapy to eradicate. And as much as it broke Bliss's heart, she wasn't sure that Maria would ever be able to integrate back into society. The isolation Maria had endured would haunt her forever. Which had made the discovery of her disappearance a triple shock. Maria went into sensory overload with minor stimulation from outdoor light and sound. How was she going to handle the stress of being out in the world alone? She needed protection from the basic triggers of everyday life.

The case had been a challenge from start to finish. And now Maria was out there somewhere. Unprotected, alone, and vulnerable. Bliss was worried sick about her.

"The idea was to place her near farms. The smells, the sounds, even the quiet is more similar to the Watsonville/ Salinas area than say, Texas." She refused to be defensive about her choices regarding Maria. But since Maria disappeared, Bliss had been second guessing every decision she'd made to keep Maria safe.

She realized maybe she hadn't completely lost the defensive in her tone when Jack's pitch black eyebrows rose. The scar crease created an interesting arch to his right brow.

"Okay." Jack shrugged. "Makes sense. But if she was relocated to Iowa, why did you have me fly here first?" Jack continued to skim through the file, looking for something, anything that would give them a lead on where Maria Torres might have gone.

"Several reasons," Jillian clipped out. "One, we wanted to makes sure you weren't followed. All we need is Fernandez getting wind of your involvement and tailing you here."

Jack started to protest, but Jill kept going. "He already knows that Maria escaped. He would have to reason that she had help when she didn't surface anywhere in California. And while there were only a few trusted people involved in her depositions, if there was even a whisper of scandal, we didn't want Fernandez to connect her with you and your company. So we didn't want the trail to lead straight to Iowa in case she is still there somewhere."

Jack stiffened. Bliss had predicted that he would be unhappy with Jill's reasons for having him come here.

She'd also told Jill to tell the truth. Jack had an aversion to lies. Jack had never said why he hated lying so much but she knew from past experience that Jack would rather have the unvarnished, uncomfortable truth than a sugar-coated lie.

Bliss smiled at Jill and encouraged her to keep going.

The delay amounted to about seven hours but now wasn't the time to cut corners. Fernandez had survived for years without detection. They had to take every precaution to keep Maria safe.

"And second?" he asked stiffly.

"We wanted to make sure you have Maria's best interests at heart."

Jack's chest broadened and his eyes narrowed. He shot a blistering glance at Bliss. "Was that your idea?" The words were gritted out through clenched teeth.

Bliss wasn't about to answer that question. Damn him. *We've met?*

Jill tried to draw Jack's attention back to her, but he didn't look away from Bliss. So finally Bliss answered carefully, "Our first priority has to be to our clients."

Which was no answer at all. But Jack's anger seemed to calm at her words as if he understood the finer points of protecting the innocent.

Jack certainly understood their motivation. Protecting clients. Protecting the innocent. He would want the same.

Judge Adams, Marsh Adams' father, had asked for Jack specifically to help track and recover Maria Torres with the Adams-Larsen team. Fortunately, before he flew out here, he'd been apprised by Jillian Larsen that the employee who arranged Maria's new life, the one who would be assisting in the recovery, was Bliss Lee. Jack's heart had nearly stopped. There couldn't be more than one Bliss Lee in the world. Half Irish, half Chinese, all female.

Jack really didn't fucking want to be here. But he'd known when Stone Consulting had an issue with the CIA and he'd used a favor from Judge Adams that he would owe the judge for taking care of it. He just hadn't thought payback would come so soon or bring up a painful, visual reminder of a time he'd tried like hell to erase from his memory banks.

Jack tried to concentrate on the file. Tried to keep his attention on the paper and words. Tried to hold on to the anger that had sustained him through the plane trip to DC. He resolutely ignored the incredible and compelling draw of Bliss.

She looked...different.

Older, of course, but in a good way. Her face had lost the slightly rounded look of youth and emphasized her Chinese heritage in the tilt of her pale, honey brown eyes, aristocratic cheekbones, strong nose, and wide, unsmiling mouth.

That had been the hardest memory to forget. She'd always been smiling, laughing. She'd told him once that she tried to find joy in every day, and that she tried to live up to her name. Life had certainly been full of bliss when they were together.

Her waist was slimmer and her breasts a little bigger based on the snug, revealing fit of her shirt. That was another thing. She used to be all colors and light, but the suit she wore was a bland, subdued navy, her shirt a plain white button up, as if she'd hidden her lightness behind boring clothes and somber colors. Or was it gone completely?

Bliss was now streamlined and sleek like a racehorse. Lots of curves, full breasts, gorgeous ass, not skinny, but not fat. And she moved with a sensual, serene maturity that had been missing at twenty.

Her body had lost the sweet softness that she'd wrapped around him eagerly. She'd drawn him in, given him a haven, a place to just be, without the responsibility that had been the cornerstone of his existence since the day his father left him in charge of the house and his family.

At fourteen, he'd been overwhelmed, terrified of fucking

up, and just plain scared. But he'd stepped up and taken care of his brothers and sister, and to some extent Shelley, his de facto step-mom even though she had the good sense not to marry his father.

But none of that mattered now. Now was all about protecting himself.

He needed to maintain the anger. And keep *her* angry. He'd seen her start to soften and he couldn't bear that. He needed her tough, a little mean. Because if she showed her softer side, he might start to lower his defenses. His anger had faded some in the face of her profound changes. This older, subdued Bliss was so radically different from his memories, he couldn't afford to give in to the urge to touch her, hold her, talk to her.

Jack shook off the need to ask her what had happened to her. This wasn't about him. Or her. He needed to focus on the case they needed to solve and leave the memories and the questions about what happened to her behind.

This was about Maria Torres. "Are you sure she left Iowa of her own accord?"

"Video surveillance of the ATM machines where she withdrew the money and the store security cameras don't show anyone with her. We analyzed her facial patterns using a cutting edge technology that measures infrared body temps and reactions and she showed no signs of undue stress. She acted furtive, nervous, skittish, but not afraid." Bliss clipped out. Her melodious voice had gone flat, monotone.

"And you're sure that Fernandez knows she escaped the house where he'd held her imprisoned?"

"He definitely knows she's gone. He's circling the wagons. He's back in California, and based on some cell phone taps from this morning he's looking to tie up loose

ends." Bliss continued to recite facts in a bland, even voice. "He used his receptionist's cell phone to call someone and order them to observe and apprehend a link to his problem."

"How do you know it was him?"

"Voice recognition software."

"How'd you get the taps on associates phones?"

Bliss kept silent.

Jack snapped his fingers. Judge Adams was one of the few who knew exactly what Fernandez was accused of and he was the one who asked Jack to help here. "Judge Adams."

She gave a little tilt to her head but didn't verbally acknowledge his guess any other way.

"You still have the tapes?"

Bliss nodded.

"Great. Can I listen to them later?"

"I'll get you a transcript. Good enough?"

Jack responded. "Fine."

"Do we know who he called?"

"No. They were using a burner phone." Bliss said, "We could pinpoint their general location from triangulating the cell towers the call bounced off but we don't have any idea of their identities. Fernandez was careful not to use any names."

Jillian Larsen tapped out a text on her smart phone. "Something urgent with another client just came up. I'm going to leave this to you two."

Bliss's head shot up from where she was reviewing documents and for one brief moment, Jack saw panic in her eyes. Then he blinked and whatever he thought he saw was replaced by the same bland, unsmiling face that she had been projecting since he walked in.

But what if her indifference to him, to everything, was all a disguise? An act?

Jack felt the uncontrollable urge to shake her up. To rattle that calm facade and see what came tumbling out. To see if that blast of panic was real. "I was ready seven hours ago. I'm just waiting on the expert, Ms. Lee."

Larsen aimed a fierce look at Jack. "Put aside your issues and work together. This is an important witness."

Jack bristled. "Believe me I have a vested interest in this guy. He pissed in my backyard." Besides the fact that he had a favor to repay to Judge Adams, the opportunity to give Ava peace of mind burned like a fire in his gut.

"Excellent." Jillian sauntered to the door of her office and glanced back one more time. "This situation needs to have a happy conclusion."

She closed the door with a muffled thump. And Jack and Bliss were alone for the first time in thirteen years.

CHAPTER 3

Suddenly the silence was laden with tension. Jack needed to hold onto his anger. But it was hard to stay angry in the face of her obvious changes when what he really wanted to do was ask her what had happened to her. But that was far too personal a topic for the strangers they were now.

Anger. Anger. Anger. He tried to channel the anger so he could stay immune to the underlying sorrow that he sensed in her. "So Fernandez knows she's escaped. Do you think he has any idea that Adams-Larsen was involved in relocating her?"

"Most people are unaware that we do anything but PR and image consulting." Bliss ran one long elegant finger over a line of type in the report. "We've maintained a ninety-nine percent success rate with our clients by being overly cautious."

Jack had been briefed by Judge Adams, Marsh Adams's father, about the other more secretive services that the company offered. But it had been a very short and succinct recitation. They relocated witnesses and people in mortal danger and gave them new lives where they could be safe. "So I'm a special case."

She jerked involuntarily before she could control the movement. "Yes. That information is usually very high clearance and individual case basis. And normally you wouldn't need to know." Bliss kept her attention on the reports. "But Fernandez has resources in high places, and if he is aware of our...other business, then anything we put online or over the airwaves could be tracked."

Jack agreed.

"I think we should go completely radio silent on this." Bliss finally held his gaze for one long fraught moment.

She wanted him to cut contact with his office. His first instinct was to argue, but then he thought about the fact that Ava had slim ties to the missing woman Maria Torres. And the fact that he had Connor looking into Fernandez's background. Maybe Bliss had a point.

"I have my brother digging for any information he can uncover on Fernandez." Jack figured they needed to share information and now was the wrong time to hold back. "What if he needs to contact me with information?"

"Phones off." She crossed her arms over her chest, the move plumped her breasts slightly, the hint of cleavage only a shadow in the V of her button up shirt. "No compromise. Maria's life is at stake. You're talking about a guy who had no qualms about leaving her trapped in a basement for *eight* years."

Jack swallowed. "So...." If they had no contact with anyone else, it meant the two of them would be working extremely closely together.

"It's just you and me," she said grimly.

Him and Bliss. A hitch of some emotion he refused to name constricted his chest.

He needed to remind himself that there was no him and Bliss for the long term. Just in the context of this case for a very short period of time they would have to work together. Distance. Perspective. Focus on her new life. *That didn't include you, you dumbass.*

She'd clearly done just fine. Without him.

Jack's blood pressure rose. Stress and worry pushed at his skull from the inside. Fuck. He did not need to pursue that line of thinking. Business. Keep his focus on business.

"Is Maria your typical client?"

"I can safely say that I've never had to relocate someone who has been basically held hostage for eight years in a basement, who never saw the light of day, or anyone besides her captors."

Jack bent forward in the fancy brocade chair, the more delicate frame groaned as he shifted his two hundred and fifty pound bulk. He bunched his fists and scowled. "That bastard."

"Yes. Which is why we need to find Maria before he does," Bliss returned solemnly.

Jack was in complete agreement. "Where do you think she went?" He leaned closer to her and her jasmine perfume teased his senses.

Bliss subtly leaned back in her chair, increasing the distance between them. "That's it. I don't have a clue." Jack could see that she was beating herself up over the fact that she couldn't intuit what Maria had been thinking. "I should have had some idea that she didn't trust us. I should have realized that she was going to bolt."

For a few seconds she clearly forgot he was in the office with her, her honey-colored gaze far off and unfocused. "Dammit. I should have known."

"But you don't have any personal experience with a total

relocation," Jack argued. He couldn't stand to see that anguished look in her eyes. "You shouldn't beat yourself up."

Bliss's expression froze for a fraction of second. Her eyes widened, and then she blinked until the fan of her lashes hid her from his suddenly far more interested gaze. And then she curved back into the wings of the chair as if very subtly hiding.

Everything in Jack tightened, sharpened, narrowed in on Bliss and her reactions. He saw beneath her outward show of frustration before she relaxed carefully. Denial. She did have experience with relocation.

His Bliss had had another identity. If he'd read her body language correctly, she'd had the kind of identity and relocation that meant she'd been witness to or had direct experience with a violent situation that she needed to be protected from. And she'd never mentioned it the entire time they'd been together.

Jack's brain kept circling around to one thought. She had experience with relocation. Questions bombarded his brain at Mach speed. When? Why? How? Where?

But Jack wasn't an idiot. If he asked her outright, she'd deny and shut him down. But what if her experience could help them figure out what Maria was doing, where she was going? Shit.

He had to shove that revelation to the back of his mind. Take it out and examine the ramifications later. Right now his focus needed to be on finding Maria. "Did you take her to Iowa personally?"

Bliss seemed to relax when she thought her reaction had dodged his notice. Far from the case, but Jack had to time his questions and come at her with them when her guard was down and she wasn't expecting them in order to get an honest answer out of her.

"Yes," Bliss admitted.

"And how was she?"

"Terrified of the sun."

"Terrified?" Jack asked skeptically.

"Honestly, she hadn't been outside in eight years." Bliss said angrily, "*Eight years*. She was afraid of everything. She'd been completely isolated, no interactions with anyone."

"What about her captors?"

"They shoved food at her through a cat door installed in the ceiling."

"Medical?"

"If she got sick they bought her over the counter medicine." Bliss rubbed her palms over her biceps. "Fortunately she seems to be extremely healthy."

"Exercise?"

"They gave her an exercise bike, a television, and a small refrigerator, and a single burner."

"Jesus." Jack rubbed his severed brow with his index finger and contemplated that information. "So where the hell would she go?"

"I don't know." Bliss tapped the gnawed end of her pen on the manila folder with all the details of Maria's case. "That's why I didn't think we'd have to worry about her taking off."

Jack stared at a pair of etchings of colonial era buildings stacked on the wall. "Are we sure she didn't just barricade herself in the basement?"

"There's a basement and a storm cellar. We inspected them thoroughly once we realized she was gone."

"How long did it take before she bolted?"

"Only a few hours." Bliss grimaced, her brows crimped

in concern. "Her large cash withdrawal at the ATM triggered an alarm in our system. I called her right away but she didn't answer. And the guard we'd placed in town was at the ATM within ten minutes."

Jack raised his eyebrows. "You provided the cell?"

Bliss said, "Yes. But her cell phone hasn't moved. She left it at the safe house."

"Who would she call?" Jack tried to approach the problem analytically. But he kept getting caught up on one fact. If he was in trouble he could call any one of his siblings and they'd drop everything to help him out. And he'd do the same for them. But Maria Torres had been alone, abandoned, for what probably felt like forever. "She didn't need the phone. She's been alone for eight years. It wouldn't occur to her that she had anyone on the other end who gave a shit."

Bliss's mouth curved downward as Jack's words hit home. "I gave a shit," she replied softly.

"I get that." Jack resisted the urge to take her in his arms and comfort her. "But she probably didn't believe you."

Bliss's eyes were glassy as she blinked rapidly.

Jack desperately tried to distract her before she started crying. "If she's been underground and isolated for the last eight years, how did she know what to do?"

"She was addicted to crime shows." Bliss's lips quirked. "CSI was her favorite."

Jack leaned forward, elbows on his knees, fingers clasped together and hung low between his spread legs as he reasoned out Maria's plans. "She couldn't possibly have figured out how to escape and evade someone like Fernandez."

"She's smart, Jack," Bliss countered. "She basically watched television and she learned."

"But this guy has been fooling the public and his staunch supporters for eight years without even a whiff of corruption or criminal activity." Jack stood and stretched his legs. He needed to be doing rather than sitting. "This situation is going to send serious shock waves through the community. Especially the Hispanic community. The guy is practically a saint in my town."

Bliss snorted. As if she couldn't restrain her curiosity any longer, she asked, "What are you doing in Monterey?"

Jack raised a brow. "I live there."

Clearly she hadn't been following up on him. Apparently not like he'd been keeping track of her.

"In Monterey?"

"Yeah." He rubbed his palm over the back of his neck trying to ease the tension that had gripped him since this morning when he'd discovered that not only was he going to have to see Bliss again but he'd have to work closely with her.

And now it appeared that while he had kept tabs on her, where she was and what she was doing, even when she'd been married, dammit, she had not given him another thought once she kicked him out of her life.

If that didn't deflate his ego faster than an inflatable pierced by a machine gun round, he didn't know what would. "I started my own company about a year ago."

"That's...great." But her face had slipped back into that mask, as if she'd shut down the monitor and turned off the lights.

"Yeah." Jack was proud of what he and his family had accomplished in one short year. "Global Humanitarian Relief has managed to do a lot of good in a very short amount of time."

"So what does this situation have to do with a humanitarian relief company?"

"I'm paying back a favor," Jack replied shortly. He wasn't about to admit any more than that. And they were wasting time. As much as he hated to take second chair, his job was muscle and resources. So he figuratively bit his tongue and deferred to Bliss. "So what's the plan?"

She raised a single brow in question.

"You're lead." Jack shrugged. "I'll follow, and offer my opinion, if requested."

"We need to figure out where she was headed." Bliss rubbed her fingers over her mouth, worry etched in every line of her face. But Jack's attention was riveted on her lips, on the sweet bow of her mouth. "Which could freaking be anywhere in the U.S."

"No passport?"

"No. We didn't give her a passport card. Thank goodness. Otherwise we'd have to expand our search to Canada and Mexico."

Jack was pretty impressed. The girl had cojones. He'd give her that. "Wouldn't she know that the safest thing she could do would be to stay put and wait until we could expose Fernandez?"

"She probably felt like she'd exchanged one prison for another." Bliss's shoulders slumped.

God, he couldn't stand to see her obvious discouragement. Without thinking, he reached over and curled his fingers around hers. The spark was instant and electric. A current shot from his fingers to his groin and his heart began to beat in triple time as if he'd been shocked by a defibrillator.

At the surprising arousal, he tightened his fingers over hers. Unwilling to let the contact slip away, he tugged her to her feet and curled his other arm around her shoulders. Bliss stiffened. But Jack was lost in the feel of her in his arms. She fit as if she'd never left. As if she'd been made just for him. Her head tucked perfectly beneath his six foot five frame and into the curve of his neck.

Jack closed his eyes, shut out the fancy office, and reveled in how she felt in his arms. Familiar, and yet different. He remembered the days when she belonged there. *Why the hell had he ever let her go?*

Except the truth was, he hadn't let her go. She'd kicked him out and never looked back. She'd gotten married. He'd celebrated the day with a highball glass and a bottle of scotch. And when she'd gotten divorced he'd spent that day the same way.

And damned himself for still caring.

Yet, all that was forgotten the moment she nestled in his arms like she'd been made just for him. She relaxed into the curve of his embrace for a precious second as if she were happy to be there. Just as happy as he was to have her there. But that quickly ended.

"What are you doing?" She shoved out of his embrace, avoiding his gaze. But her indifferent mask had slipped revealing a pain she'd hidden expertly. Her anguish nearly brought him to his knees with its depth and intensity. But then he realized she'd been hiding things for years.

He thought about her hesitation when he'd said she wouldn't have any personal knowledge of relocation and witness protection. Her reaction meant she'd been keeping secrets for far longer than he could even imagine. That was irrelevant right now.

But in the back of his mind, where all this new information about Bliss took up residence and simmered, he wondered...What else had she hidden from him?

"You need to stop beating yourself up over this."

"Really?" Bliss's bland mask disappeared in a puff of anger. Her honey eyes sparkled and her face heated. The indifference was gone.

Jack could feel himself getting sucked back in to the vortex that was Bliss Lee. He couldn't afford to let her get to him. He'd been lost the last time she'd tossed him out. While he liked to think he was older, wiser, and his heart protected by a cynical barrier that not much penetrated anymore, he wasn't about to chance it and end up devastated and alone in the same position thirteen years later. The thought that she could suck him in and he would end up back in the same place raised his ire.

"Fine. Let's just focus on what to do next." Anger was a much easier emotion to express than regret and sorrow, so Jack embraced the geyser of hurt and rage that shot up from the pit of his stomach and jabbed at her with a small dig. "What would you have done?"

Bliss jerked as if he'd punched her, but she didn't acknowledge that he'd scored a direct hit. She shut her eyes and contemplated what her response would have been to a threat. What action would her instinct prod her to take?

"The first primal instinct is to get as far away from...Fernandez as possible." Bliss rubbed her palms against her biceps, the gesture caused the button up shirt to gap. Jack tried to keep his gaze from drifting to the tantalizing glimpse of skin. "That was part of the reason I put her in Iowa, besides the smells and sounds."

"What?"

"It's smack in the middle between California and DC." Bliss lamented, "I wanted her to feel safe."

Bliss paced around the office until she stood behind the wing chair. The furniture was like a shield that protected her

body from his penetrating stare. Her fingers traced the graceful arch of the back as she processed her thoughts.

"What's the second?" Because if Maria was as smart as Bliss thought, then she wouldn't go with instinct number one.

"Go back," Bliss whispered.

"What?"

Bliss tilted her head, her burnished copper hair fell over one shoulder. "Where's the last place he would look for her?"

Jack shook his head. "She wouldn't."

"It's what I would do." Bliss argued as the idea took root. And she knew with the instincts that had protected her for the last eighteen years, that she was right. "She's got guts. She'd go back to the absolute last place Fernandez would look for her."

Jack was speechless.

"We've got to go. Now."

"Where are we going?" Jack asked.

"California," Bliss said grimly. "After a quick stop in Iowa."

CHAPTER 4

Shane had filed their flight plan and was doing the preflight check on the Bombardier while Jack got Bliss settled. Once Bliss was ensconced in a butter soft, cream leather seat in the passenger cabin of the Stone family jet, Jack went to the cockpit and sat with Shane, serving as the co-pilot for takeoff.

It had been a long fucking day.

But Jack bet the day had been even longer for Maria Torres. Wherever she was.

He was torn between wanting to spend more time with Bliss and wanting to stay as far away from her as possible. But he had a duty to Maria, a responsibility to the people, to find her and make sure that José Fernandez paid for his actions eight years ago.

So once they were airborne, Jack reluctantly said, "I'm going to go check on our passenger. Be back in a bit."

Shane wiggled his brows and his wide smile was blindingly bright in his dark, ebony face. "Lucky you." He laughed low and melodic as Jack unbuckled and headed for his passenger.

"I wish," he muttered. Not lucky, cursed.

Jack closed the curtain between the cockpit and the cabin and took a second to soak her in. She was searching through papers on the burled wood table between the seats, seemingly absorbed in the paperwork scattered across the surface. He noted the tiny wrinkle between her eyebrows, and the way she still nibbled on the end of her pen when she concentrated intently.

A pang of nostalgia hit him hard. How many times had he teased her about those damn pens? How many times had he tried to give her something else to nibble on? And how many times had he convinced her to nibble on him?

Jack needed to remember the bad things. Not the good. She'd ripped out his heart and stomped on it when she'd ended their relationship. That's what he needed to remember.

He'd been speculating about where Maria might go, or who she might go to when she left the safe house, but he realized he'd forgotten one element.

"What about family?" Jack said abruptly.

But Bliss didn't answer. Then he noticed the wires hanging from her ears. She had her headphones on and couldn't hear him. Another memory bombarded him. He used to get her attention by kissing her out of a study trance.

No kissing. He licked his lips and shoved the memories aside. Instead he strode over to her and stood in front of her until she looked up and removed the earbuds. "Yes?"

"What about family?"

Bliss wrapped the wires around the small iPod mini meticulously as she took her time answering. "Her parents were heartbroken when she disappeared. They went back to their home town in Mexico. Her father was killed a year later, caught in the wrong place during a drug war battle. Her mother...isn't well."

"Is the mother coming back to the States?"

"We're trying to get her here but it doesn't look good? Why?"

"So there's no one else that would be vulnerable to Fernandez and possibly in danger?"

"Not so far as I know. A close friend, or a mentor might be in danger if Fernandez thought that he could get to Maria by pulling them in and using them as leverage." Bliss was analytical and almost emotionally detached. "But let's face it, she hasn't been around for eight years. I doubt anyone thinks of her any more as anything other than a tragic memory."

There was a distinct lack of emotion in both her tone and her face, which pissed Jack off. She was the one who lost her. Maria was the client. Didn't she feel the slightest bit responsible? Jack was practically climbing the walls with the lack of progress on finding Maria and she'd only been his client for about twelve hours.

But then he realized Bliss's lack of emotion hid a profound sadness. And he wanted to ask...who didn't miss you?

Jack couldn't dwell on that right now. He had to get his head back into this mission. He thought about Bliss's assessment of who could be a target. He knew someone who missed Maria. Someone who'd remodeled her entire life after her friend disappeared. A cold fear spread through Jack.

"Fuck."

"What's wrong?"

"My assistant, Ava, was Maria's best friend." Jack informed her.

"That's awfully coincidental," Bliss said suspiciously. Jack didn't understand the edge of animosity beneath her very flat monotone.

"How do you mean?"

"Your assistant is connected to the missing witness." Bliss said calmly, "How did you become a part of this search again?"

"I owed Judge Adams a favor. That's why he called me and because he knew that Fernandez is a large political force in my area. He's also aware of the relationship between Ava and Maria."

"Again, coincidental."

"Not really." Jack shook his head. "I hired her because of her experiences, her empathy and her need to atone. She has the perfect mindset for GHR."

"Ah yes, the philanthropic arm of your business." Bliss crossed her arms over her chest. "What about Stone Consulting? Is she perfect for that business too? Because the quiet word on the street is that Stone Consulting can get sensitive intel and has a knack for jobs that require...discretion."

Jack wondered how she knew that but now wasn't the time to talk about his other business. "That's not relevant."

"It is if you're working for Fernandez."

"What?" Jack couldn't even figure how she could make that accusation. "Jesus. I'm not working for Fernandez."

"It had to be asked."

"You have balls," Jack muttered. "I'll give you that."

"I don't need you to give me anything," Bliss snarled.

Except an explanation apparently. "Judge Adams called in a favor and asked me to help out since he knows about my connection to this case." Jack was annoyed that he even had to explain himself. His temper simmered at the suggestion that he was dirty. When had he ever given her the impression that he would turn out that way? Staying angry, rather than succumbing to poignant memories and old regrets, wasn't going to be a problem. Calming down might.

"Could your assistant, Ava, somehow tip Fernandez off?"

"Not a chance. I didn't tell anyone where I was going, or what I was working on." Jack took a deep breath. "Let's focus on the issue at hand. Ava is a link."

"Eight years ago, Jack." Bliss waved her fingers. "Honestly, she wasn't in a position of power then and she isn't now either."

"I would still like to warn Ava to be on the lookout for anything unusual."

"Absolutely not." Bliss was adamant. "The first rule of successful relocation with a new identity is no contact with your former life. The key to hiding is to completely change your way of life. So take that to the next level for protecting Maria. You need to pretend Ava never knew Maria. You cannot take the risk that if you bring up Maria that Ava won't mention it to someone. Because someone, somewhere might be listening."

"But—"

"Right now, Fernandez has a prisoner that's escaped but absolutely no leads on where she went."

"How did she get to Adams-Larsen?"

"She is blessed with unbelievable luck."

"Except for that whole being imprisoned for eight years," Jack snarked.

"Fine. But when she escaped, she scrambled through a canyon and went to the nearest house. Turns out the owner is a former U.S. Marshal." Bliss chewed on the pen tip.

"Although he'd never done a stint in Wit Sec, he had friends who are still in the service. So he knew exactly what to do."

"So why didn't she stay with the marshals?"

"Marshals protect federal witnesses. There's no trial, or even technical threat against her yet. The case against Fernandez doesn't exist yet. So she isn't eligible for protection right now. Once she testifies against Fernandez, she can go into the witness protection if she wishes."

Right, so her life can be taken away again. How many times was this poor girl going to be ripped away from everything she'd ever known? Jack shook off that worry. Right now he needed information.

And Bliss still didn't answer his question on how Maria ended up in DC at Adams-Larsen. "So how did she get to you?"

"Both Jill and Marsh are former marshals," Bliss said. "Luckily, the neighbor's contact knew about the other side of Adams-Larsen's business."

"So it really was a series of lucky events that brought Maria Torres to you?" Jack mused. "I guess her luck is changing."

"A series of unbelievably lucky events." Bliss frowned. "So why did she run?"

CHAPTER 5

They got to the isolated farm house an hour and a half after they landed at the Perry Municipal Airport outside Des Moines. The dark night was unbroken only by one large spotlight strung up at the top of a single bare post. It illuminated the front yard and the steps leading up to the rickety old porch.

Jack withdrew his weapon from his belt holster as they cautiously approached the weathered structure. Peeling paint revealed patches of bare, worn wood and a tangle of brush surrounded the base of the house.

Crickets chirped, frogs croaked in the immense silence. No cars traveled the deserted two lane road, and the howl of a coyote pack haunted the waning moonlit night. The stars sparkled in the still sky. Frost crystallized on the bare grass. Winter was edging in the barren farm town.

From the road the house looked deserted, half overgrown with brambles and old bushes that hadn't been trimmed for years. One of the shutters had lost a hinge and hung crooked against the peeling wood siding, but a shiny new industrial lock gleamed through the dark shadows of the unlit porch.

"It's straight out of a horror flick," Jack commented mildly.

"It's isolated and unregistered. The land belongs to a trust, so it's almost impossible to trace."

Jack tilted his head to the side and indicated that Bliss move behind him. She rolled her eyes but before she could argue, he knocked on the door, the bang loud in the quiet air.

Bliss huffed out an annoyed breath, stepped around him, and smoothly inserted the key into the well-oiled lock. She turned the knob and stepped into the darkened foyer before Jack could stop her.

"Maria?" Bliss called out. Just in case she had gone back to the house. But there was no answer, no sound at all but the hum of the refrigerator and the distinct smell of something rotting.

Jack grabbed Bliss by the bicep and held on tightly. "Wait."

He braced for what they might find and flipped on the light switch in the entry. But what greeted them was...nothing. There wasn't a thing out of place. A simple sofa, coffee table, and television were the only items in the stark living room.

They stalked cautiously into the kitchen, empty except for a plain square table and two beat up wood chairs. A package of hamburger meat sat forgotten on the chipped Formica countertop—likely the source of the rotting smell— a dirty coffee cup rested in the scratched stainless steel sink, and an empty metal sauce pan sat on the old burner. The faded floral curtains over the window sink were pulled shut casting the room in darkness except for a sliver of moonlight.

But that was it.

The rest of the house was pristine.

In the bedroom, the double bed had been made with the covers pulled precisely tight and the comforter smoothed. In the bathroom, a few cosmetics littered the tiny faux-marble vanity top. And shampoo and conditioner sat like little soldiers on the lip of the worn ceramic tub.

In the closet, a variety of clothes, simple cotton dresses and sweat pants and sweatshirts hung carefully straight, some with the tags still on them. Even in the battered dresser, underwear and socks were folded and put away neatly. But she was still gone.

For a second, Bliss's shoulders slumped. "She really is gone."

"Bright side. No signs of forced entry, no signs that she was attacked, or abducted."

Bliss glanced around the bedroom one more time. "Looks like she left without taking anything with her. Except what she was wearing."

"However the hamburger on the counter suggests she took off impulsively."

"And didn't know she wouldn't be back?" Bliss straightened her shoulders.

"Hard to tell." Jack said, "But even if she thought that Fernandez had found her, she wasn't harmed here. And based on your video surveillance she withdrew money and bought goods without being under duress."

Bliss tightened her mouth as she surveyed the old, rundown farmhouse one more time.

"These are all good signs." Jack felt compelled to try to cheer her up.

"Yeah, but I didn't figure on her running." Bliss fingered the bottle of perfume on the old vanity. "At all."

Jack was quiet. He didn't know this new Bliss. And he wasn't sure what he could say to help. If anything. With a sense of dread, he asked, "You want to talk about it?"

"About what?" She crossed her arms over her chest in a classic defensive body language.

"The fact that you have psychological knowledge of what someone who is in protection would feel, what they would do."

"Years of working with them," she tossed out far too quickly.

Jack was surprised at the stab of disappointment he felt when she didn't even pretend to give a truthful answer. Which was stupid. What was the end game of knowing more about her? Nothing. There was no end game. He just needed to get through this assignment, find Maria Torres, then they could go back to their separate coasts.

And he could go back to...whatever.

"Let's clean up the kitchen and we'll find a place to crash for the night." His tone was abrupt, chilly.

"We can't leave for Monterey now?"

Jack shared her impatience but they needed to follow FAA protocol. Not to mention the fact that their pilot was over a hundred miles away. "Shane needs a mandated rest before getting in the air again. Plus, he went to visit a buddy the opposite direction from here. He'll be at the airport and ready to go first thing in the morning. We can get an early start tomorrow."

"Actually, since we aren't tied to a commercial schedule, we should check out the places that Maria visited and see if anyone else has been asking about her." Bliss sighed. "So we'll need to wait until the stores open tomorrow anyway."

They headed downstairs to the kitchen. Jack scooped the package of ground beef into the garbage and then tied the bag up and lifted it out of the plastic can from underneath the sink. "I'll take this out to the dumpster."

Bliss followed behind Jack and locked the door while he headed around the back of the house.

Jack lifted the lid on the small battered dumpster and started to toss the bag. But the flutter of a newspaper caught his eye. No recycling out here. There were no other bags of garbage inside. And he wondered why the paper would already be in the dumpster. Why would Maria have gone to the trouble to throw the paper away in there?

He leaned into the stinky, metal container and grabbed the paper. He didn't even have it halfway out when the headline caught his eye. Jack let the lid slam shut and hustled to the car.

Bliss was already in the driver's seat.

"I think I found why she ran."

He held up the paper. The headline read: *Fernandez a Shoe In for Top Labor Job*.

WHO COULD HAVE PREDICTED that the Holiday Arts and Crafts Fair would be such a draw that all the hotel rooms in the surrounding eighty miles would be booked?

Bliss cursed all those crafty people out there. They were turning her life into a nightmare. She'd thought she'd at least have the night to regroup after spending the last seven hours in her former lover's company. Instead they were forced to share a room. And they were lucky they'd found this one. For a while it had been looking like they were going to be sleeping in their rental car.

They had needed to pay cash, which also limited their sleeping options. They were lucky they found this dump. The wallpaper adorned with tractors and wheat fields in earth tones and bronze metallics, the starburst clock on the wall, and the brown shag carpeting were about twenty years out of date. But it did have two beds for which she was grateful.

She needed a damn break.

The toilet flushed in the miniscule hotel bathroom and Bliss slid under the rough, cheap cotton sheets before Jack came out of the bathroom.

Bliss was trying hard to ignore the fact that was she was in a hotel room with Jack Stone. He'd been the yardstick for every other man she'd been intimate with, and now with him so close again, she wondered, was it just 'first love' memories?

Jack burst out of the bathroom like he was being attacked and Bliss jerked. She'd forgotten how everything he did was physically imposing. He moved and breathed and sucked the air from the universe.

Jack was big. But more than that, he had a big personality. He commanded attention. Not in an overt way but somehow when Jack was around he drew energy from the air and it nearly crackled around him.

Of course he noticed her flinch. "You okay?"

"Besides that fact that I'm sorta wishing I had a black light for these sheets—"

Jack snorted. "No, you don't."

"I'm...fine."

The tension in the room ramped up to a new height as the reality that they were in a hotel room together seemed to hit them at the both time. All day Bliss had been trying to ignore his innate sex appeal. Jack had always been a tactile person. He liked to touch, to stroke, to feel. He'd spent hours exploring her skin, her curves, her mouth seemingly never tired of just…learning her body.

He'd taken off his t-shirt and stripped down to a pair of basketball shorts. Jack ran hot. She'd never needed a blanket when they slept together, his body was like a raging inferno. He'd kept her warm and safe wrapped in his arms. At least she'd felt safe.

An illusion, but back then she still had nightmares and sometime the old fear would sneak up on her while she slept. But Jack had made all those fears disappear when he held her in his arms. The feeling of safety had let her sleep at night. And when he'd left, she'd gone back to her sleepless, restless nights for a long time. Until she'd learned to keep herself safe.

But oh, those nights in his embrace. The way his much larger frame dwarfed hers. The way he put his body between hers and the door. The way he'd made her feel safe without even knowing that he'd given her that gift.

Bliss's breath caught as memories bombarded her. "Night." She rolled over quickly and faced the hideous ancient wallpaper.

Jack slid into the other bed. She heard the rustle of the sheets, and the squeak of the box springs as he propped up the pillows and pulled out the file regarding Maria and flipped through the sheaf of papers. They had gone completely old school with Maria. Her name wasn't anywhere in the Adams-Larsen database so there was no way for anyone to hack their system and find information. He sipped from the water bottle next to the bed.

Bliss was exhausted. But the emotional toll of the last few hours hit her hard and her brain wouldn't shut off. She kept seeing the hard planes of Jack's chest, the ripple of his pectorals and the bunch of his biceps as he crossed his arms over his massive chest.

Bliss's breath came faster and she began to sweat as other images of Jack bombarded her. His fierce determination to protect his assistant. His frustration when they'd found the house empty. His relief when they found no evidence of foul play at the safe house. The longing that she managed to suppress most days came roaring to the forefront of her mind. She missed his passion. Missed his intensity, missed him.

She needed to shut down that line of thinking right damn now.

She just needed to get through the next few days, find Maria as quickly as possible, then Jack Stone would be gone, and her life could go back to normal. She could hold out. She just needed to focus on Maria. On getting her back.

And then she would be lonely again.

BLISS WAS FINALLY ASLEEP. He'd listened to her panicked breath and wondered what she had been thinking about?

But he was no longer entitled to that knowledge. He'd given up the right to be privy to her thoughts right around the time he'd left. Although in reality, she'd kicked him out.

To put it mildly, he'd been shocked when she'd told him they were over. Completely blind-sided. Thankfully, he'd already joined the Navy and he'd known it was the right move. She had never explained why she had dumped him. But even if it had something to do with his intention to serve, he wouldn't have given it up. He'd given up his childhood to take care of his step-mother and siblings. He'd been responsible for everyone for years. He'd known that the

Navy was his path. That he needed, wanted, someone else to be in charge, at least for a little while.

When they'd been together, life had been amazing. He'd left California, his brothers and sister behind and reveled in his newfound freedom. He hadn't been responsible for anyone but himself. And yes, he had felt guilty off and on. He'd done what he wanted, when he wanted it, and only thought about how Shelley and the kids had been getting along in the dark of the night, when he couldn't sleep or the quiet morning dawn when his head had been pounding from a hangover and too little sleep.

Jack continued to sift through the files. He just needed to get through this, find Maria, and get back to the West Coast and forget all about Bliss. But he knew after less than a day in her presence that was going to be easier said than done. Jack tried to wipe the memory of the fear on her face when they'd first gone into that house earlier.

She'd been terrified that they were going to find Maria dead. The stench of the rotting meat wasn't distinguishable from other types of rotting flesh. She'd known instinctively that something was dead, which also made him wonder what she'd seen in her life.

Jack glanced over to her bed, stared hard at the elegant curve of her back and the tumble of her auburn hair on the pillow and tried not to remember when that hair had cascaded over his chest and shoulders. Tried not to remember waking up with her wrapped around him, curled into his body as if he were her world.

Jack forced his gaze back to the papers and his laptop. If Bliss was correct and Maria was heading back to California, to the Salinas area, and she didn't fly which required identification, how long would it take? And what would likely be her route from the middle of the country to the

West Coast? Several days. Within an hour of withdrawing the cash, she'd would have been on the road. There were so many variables with all the unknowns. Car, bus, train? The bus and the train would take less time than driving a car. If she drove herself, she'd have to stop to sleep. So bus or train would likely mean she'd get to California sometime Sunday. If she drove it would take longer.

Bliss's body twitched, and drew his gaze back to her.

Jack frowned. He watched her for another moment, then returned to his examination of possible avenues for Maria to travel.

Bliss's entire body jerked as if she'd been shot, then she whimpered and jerked again.

Jack swallowed. Nightmare? Bad dream?

"Bliss," he whispered. But she didn't react to his whispered attempt to wake her up.

Her whimpers degenerated into soft cries as she twitched, jerked against invisible bonds or imaginary attacks.

Fuck.

"Bliss." This time he spoke in a normal voice and still she didn't awaken.

Jack sighed and moved his laptop and papers to the side. He did not want to go over to her bed. He could only take so much.

But as her cries got louder, he realized he had to stop her dream, nightmare, whatever. She was caught in some scenario that was causing her great distress.

Jack shoved the covers aside and knelt on Bliss's bed, one knee planted behind her back, his other foot on the floor. He placed his palm on her hunched shoulder. "Bliss."

Dammit. He tried not to notice the smooth skin of her shoulder and the sweet scent of jasmine shampoo as he touched her flesh for the first time in thirteen years.

But when she didn't wake, Jack bent over her body and leaned down and began to speak quietly, "Bliss, wake up."

His hand on her shoulder must have triggered another fight or flight response, because Bliss rolled onto her back and began to struggle in earnest. "No, no, no, no," she murmured.

Jack's heart iced. What the hell was she dreaming about? "Bliss, wake up."

She flailed her arms and Jack grabbed her wrists so she didn't accidentally hurt herself. Tears trailed down her face. At this point, Jack had one knee planted by her waist and the other foot on the floor, but his torso was even with hers and whenever she bucked trying to get him off, her breasts brushed his chest. His cheek was even with hers as he spoke calmly, deliberately in her ear, repeating the words over and over again, "You're okay. I've got you."

Jack tensed as she continued to struggle. He kept repeating the assurances. "Bliss, you're okay. I've got you."

Finally, she stopped struggling and gave a shuddering breath. Jack leaned back just in time to see her spiky wet lashes flutter open. He still held her wrists lightly trying to make sure she didn't hurt herself.

"I've got you."

"Jack?" Her honey eyes were glazed and she still seemed disoriented.

"I've got you." Jack curbed the urge to tell her he'd always have her.

"It's you." She threw herself against him and twined her arms around his body so tightly he had to shift to draw breath. "It's you."

Bliss pressed frantic kisses to his ear, his cheek, arrowing toward his mouth. Jack was shocked speechless. So much so that when she pressed her lips to his, he didn't immediately stop her.

Bliss had risen to her knees and pressed her body tight against his. And she felt so right , so familiar against him that Jack let himself return the kiss. Like all was perfect with the universe, she melted against him, her arms tight around his neck, her breasts pillowed against his chest, her fingers gripped his hair and pulled him closer as if she never wanted to let him go. Jack's cock responded to the stimulus and he swelled with need, with love.

Jack got caught in the memory of them pressed together, and the familiarity took his breath away.

She rubbed her body against his. Her generous breasts, a perfect handful, spilled from the pink spaghetti tank. The concave bow of her belly, clad in matching pink and tan plaid flannel shorts, cradled his erection.

She moaned at the intimate contact and fused her mouth to his. Jack lost himself in their kiss. The way they fit together, the way her mouth felt beneath his, the way her tongue stroked against his. Jack slid one hand into her hair and cupped the nape of her neck in his palm. She was so delicate. He'd forgotten because her personality was so bold, but she was more fragile, breakable than he remembered.

He gentled his hold, but Bliss wanted nothing to do with gentle. She snaked an arm around his back and clenched her fist tightly in the waistband of his basketball shorts. Her other hand gripped his ass with a desperate insistence.

In an instant, memories of him and Bliss together washed over him. And he kissed her back. Kissed her with all the pent up longing that had been building since he'd found out that he was going to see her again.

Bliss slid her hands around and gripped his biceps. With

surprising strength pulled him even closer into her embrace. "Please," she whispered. "Jack."

Jack lost himself in the fierceness of her desire. She shoved his shorts to his knees and he groaned into mouth as she wrapped her long delicate fingers around his thick, engorged shaft.

Jack's head swam. All the blood in his body zoomed to his cock as she gripped him perfectly and pumped. Dammit. She'd always had the ability to take him from zero to two hundred in seconds and apparently that hadn't gone away.

He should remove her hand. He knew she still wasn't quite aware of her surroundings. But she'd groaned his name, so she knew who she was with.

Jack cupped her face and kissed her tears away. When they'd been together before, she'd never cried. Not once. She had occasionally been melancholy but she'd never exposed a crippling weakness like that before.

Her thumb swiped over the head of his cock. Desire wept from the tip.

Jesus. He wanted her. And call him selfish but he wasn't about to stop her.

Jack smoothed his palms down her neck and pushed the spaghetti straps of her cotton camisole over her shoulders and over the beautiful globes of her breasts and then cupped her in his palms. Her nipples beaded at the exposure to the cool air and burrowed into the warmth of his palms as he explored her soft skin.

They were kneeling on the bed. Her hips rocked into his full to bursting erection, the cotton flannel soft as she rubbed against his bare thick cock.

Jack shuddered as she squeezed the root. He moaned into her mouth. She was killing him. Jack slid his palms down her flat stomach, and pushed the little plaid boxer

shorts and her panties over her hips until his fingers
hit gold.

Fuck yes. She was dripping wet as he slid his middle
finger through the nest of curls and gently, lightly rubbed
her clit.

She jerked again. But this time in arousal as her body
surrendered to his caress. Jack continued to explore her
sweet sex as he rubbed the juice of her desire over her and
through the curls. With his other hand he cupped her
rounded ass, and urged her against his erection.

She attacked his mouth, and her movements became
more frantic. Jack knew he should slow things down. Take
time to rediscover every nook, every sensitive curve, every
place that made her shiver, every hidden spot that would
ramp her up until she was begging for him to take her.

But Jack was overcome with the sensations of her
smooth palm curled around him, the urgency her hips. As
she silently begged him to finish what they started, he
couldn't seem to make himself slow down.

He bent to draw her beaded nipple into his mouth. Bliss
clutched his head to her breast and moaned.

God, her taste. Her urgency. Her need.

He needed to slow down. Make this memorable. Savor
the taste and feel of Bliss.

Fuck. Today had been insane. Seeing Bliss again
brought up all the old emotions and sorrow that he'd shoved
down into his subconscious for the last thirteen years.

"Condom?" Bliss panted.

Condom? Yes. Thank God he was prepared.

"God." Jack was nearly frantic with the need to be inside
her. To find what had been missing in his life for the past
thirteen years. "Minute."

He broke away from her embrace, pushed his shorts to

the floor and stumbled over to his duffel, felt her gaze follow him as he rummaged through his bag.

Bliss couldn't look away as he moved with purpose back toward the bed. She was fully awake now and couldn't help but appreciate the beauty of his body. Jack had filled out into all man. His shoulders were padded with muscle, his pecs a work of art, dusted with hair that lead like an arrow down his ridged belly to the nest of black curls that surrounded his erection.

His thick, engorged cock jutted from the V and bounced against his belly with each long stride. Her sex fluttered at the purpose in his gaze and another swell of desire made her light-headed as he ripped the package open and then rolled the condom over his sex.

She should stop him. Stop this. It had taken forever to get over him the last time. But really, it couldn't have been that good. Right? There was only one way to find out.

And while for years she'd been telling herself that she'd romanticized and embellished his prowess in bed, she welcomed the chance to discover if he really was as amazing as her memories made him seem.

She'd missed this, missed him. No one since Jack had made her feel this way. Empty with desperate need, as if he didn't get inside her, she would die from the lack. And he was the only one who could fill her up.

Her whole body clenched at the thought of having Jack inside her again.

Bliss tore the pale pink cami over her head and tossed it on the covers. By the time he got back to the double bed, she'd shimmied all the way out of the little plaid flannel shorts.

No hesitation. Jack came over her body. Pressed his

naked torso against hers. The head of his cock brushed against her folds and teased her clit.

But he didn't push inside. Jack propped up on his elbows, his hairy thighs abraded her softer skin, his erection nudged her sex and his ribcage pinned her to the bed. But she knew that if she said the word, he'd stop in a heartbeat.

"You sure?"

She wanted to say so many things. No, she wasn't sure. But she was sure that if they didn't do this that she'd always regret it. *Always.* "Do it."

Jack rocked his hips, and his cockhead teased at her entrance. Bliss's sex clenched as if trying to draw him in. Jack groaned. "You're so damn wet."

"So do it," she commanded.

He groaned out a laugh. "Bossy."

She hated to beg. So she nudged her hips up even as she curved her hands around his ass and pulled him closer.

Jack slid in another inch. He was so damn big. And it felt incredible. Her body had always surrendered to his invasion like the tide surrendered to the pull of the moon. "Dammit, Jack."

With his feet, he spread her legs wider, and slid all the way home.

"Oh." She sighed. He felt amazing, incredible, and she was weak with the desire coursing through her.

Jack thrust slowly, prolonging both their pleasure. With each glide the head of his cock massaged her g-spot and pushed her higher. Her whole body tingled as her head went light and her movements became more frantic. God, she needed him to push harder, faster. But with each urgent nudge of her hips, his movements became slower, more deliberate and her desire spiraled into heightened pleasure.

Bliss slid her hands around his back, held tight, and sucked at the sensitive spot below his ear. "Please."

As if her plea broke something inside him, Jack began to plunge. Each forceful thrust banged their bodies together, he swelled impossibly larger, slid his palms underneath her ass and tilted her hips until they slammed together with hard thrusts. Each thrust pushed her higher until she imploded.

Her body in free fall, she contracted around him, her vision dimmed, as her climax went on and on and on. Her channel clenched around his cock until he erupted, his back bowed, tendons in his neck straining, his hands hard on her ass, his body rigid as his orgasm wracked his body.

The pulse of his cock against her walls triggered another mini-orgasm and Bliss moaned.

A fierce sense of triumph roared through her as he slumped against her body. His forehead bumped her collarbone, the rough sough of his breath feathered across her sensitive nipples and she shivered.

Her legs loosened their grip on the back of his thighs and fell limply to the bed. They were both bathed in perspiration and slippery as he laid his head on her chest. Her heart thumped against his cheek and Bliss tenderly ran her fingers through his hair, shorter than when they lived together. She savored the heavy weight of him on top of her.

And fuck, what had she done? Because she'd been wrong. She hadn't romanticized him or the sex. It was even better than her memories.

BLISS WOKE SLOWLY. Still pitch black outside, the hotel room was bathed in shadows. The sliver of light from the bathroom cast a glow onto the brown and gold polyester

striped spread on other double bed. The other *empty* double bed.

Her body was loose and achy. Wrapped in a tight, protective embrace, an inferno of heat ran along her back and the hot band around her waist suddenly registered. Every muscle tensed. *Oh my God.*

What had she done?

Holy shit. She'd had sex with Jack Stone.

Last night's encounter freeze-framed through her mind. Jack's muscles rippling as he slid inside her. His thick, thrilling invasion. The press of his hips against her spread thighs. His perfect, heavy comforting weight as she fell asleep beneath him.

The sex had been amazing. Fantastic. Epic.

And such an incredible mistake.

She dropped her chin to her chest and fought the urge to curl up into a fetal ball. What the hell had she been thinking?

She hadn't, clearly. She'd been freaked after the nightmare. She'd been searching through the house, looking for Maria but then the dream had morphed and she'd been looking for Jack. Each successive room was empty and her panic had escalated until she'd been frantic. Until she'd found him. Dead. Her fear for him. Her fear for her sister and father. Her fear for herself and her mother. All merged into one horrific dream where her worst nightmare had come true.

Of course when she woke all the way up, she'd reached out to him. To touch him. To verify with her own hands that he was alive and healthy. The emotional impact of seeing him again, the toll of worry about Maria, dredged up all her former worries, and her brain had mixed it all up and spilled out her terror.

Last night was physical. That's all. A sexual release she hadn't gotten in a very long time. A *very* long time.

Bliss wondered how difficult it would be for her to extricate herself from his arms and go have a breakdown in the bathroom. Likely impossible. Jack had been a light sleeper years ago. She'd guess that hadn't changed.

She took stock. If she wasn't mistaken, he was already awake. And typical Jack he was assessing, holding back, waiting for her.

She had to treat this as a casual encounter. She couldn't afford to get emotionally tangled up with Jack again. The last time had nearly destroyed her.

Casual. Much needed release. She drew in a mental breath. She could do this. Pretend this wasn't some monumental joining. Project an air of nonchalance. Just two healthy people enjoying each other's bodies. Play it cool.

She patted the hand wrapped around her waist briskly and he moved his arm. Bliss slid out of bed and ignored the impulse to run for the bathroom. Instead she braced herself, turned and gave him a satisfied smile. "Morning."

"Good. Morning." His voice, gravelly and still laced with sleep, caused a rush of desire to warm her belly and flood her sex. But hell if she was going there again.

Her blood pooled in her groin but she forced herself to saunter to the bathroom slowly. Her heart pounded and sweat sheened her skin as she pretended all the way across the room.

Jack was a guy. Guys typically didn't like to talk things to death. And Jack had been less likely to talk and share than other men she'd been intimate with but she needed to say something to indicate they weren't going to talk about it. She turned at the thin, wood door, hand on the cheap faux brass knob and gave him a fake smile and stared over his shoulder. "Thanks for last night." Then she closed the door behind her.

So, that happened.

Jack considered the closed bathroom door. He'd been awake awhile. He'd just lain there and savored the feel of Bliss in his arms. It had been a long while since he'd slept with anyone. Oh, he'd had sex, but the last time he'd actually slept in the same bed with a woman had been...with Bliss.

He'd lived on base when he'd been in the Navy, even when he was with Naval Intelligence. Even after he moved off base, he never brought women to his home. He went to their place and then left before he fell asleep. Now, maybe because he lived with his mother and siblings, he didn't bring women home either. Last year when he'd moved back to Monterey to start the business, he'd moved back into the Stone Mansion and just...never moved out.

But sleeping with Bliss last night had been...amazing. She fallen asleep beneath him before he'd even gone completely soft. And when he'd come out of the bathroom after disposing of the condom, he'd stared at his bed, then at her naked form, and consciously slid under the covers and curled around her.

He hadn't been able to bear leaving her yet.

Fuck. He needed to shut that line of thinking down right now.

It was just sex. Physical release. He'd been so busy getting the company off the ground he hadn't had a lot of time for women in the last year. No way was last night as momentous as it felt at the time.

He'd felt her wake up. Felt her tense. And the disappointment that overwhelmed him had been concrete. He'd been hoping for the soft, sweet, old Bliss. Instead, he'd gotten the new, closed off, secretive Bliss and for the first time ever he wanted to talk about what had happened last night.

Jesus, he was turning into a sappy idiot.

They needed to find Maria Torres before he completely lost his balls.

He couldn't afford to get tangled up with her again. His business was going extremely well, his family was just starting to gel. Last night with Bliss was just a distraction. A way to get her out of his system once and for all.

But in the back of his mind, he wondered, what if this were a second chance?

CHAPTER 6

They were on their way back to California. Shane had met them at the Perry Regional Airport with a big smile on his face, which made Jack question his assurance that he had been hanging out with an old Army buddy last night.

Jack had avoided any personal, emotional minefields by sticking strictly to the case and spending as much time in the co-pilot chair next to Shane as possible. He had his pilot's license but usually took the flight time to work.

Shane had raised a questioning brow and looked at Jack like he was crazy. He shook his head. "You Stone brothers." Shane's deep voice echoed in his ears, the noise cancelling headphones made it easy to hear him and blocked out the sound of Bliss breathing. "You got a captive audience, and you aren't taking advantage of the opportunity."

Brothers? The only other brother Shane had flown recently was Riley. He couldn't possibly be talking about Riley and Diana Lundberg. She had shut Riley down hard when they'd met, and called Jack repeatedly, right up until the day before their trip, to try to get a different guide for her mission to Jolo Island to deliver school supplies.

But Diana was out of luck. Riley was definitely the best employee for the dangerous trip.

Too bad the headphones couldn't also put up a wall around distracting people as well. Jack was hyper-aware of Bliss in the cabin behind him. They'd left the curtain to the cockpit open, in case she needed them. Her attention was firmly on the file in her hands. Too aware. She hadn't looked up once, which told him she was trying hard to keep her attention on the papers and off everything else.

Like the fact that they'd had sex last night.

He couldn't let his mind stray there. He needed to focus on finding Maria. Because that was his job, he needed to forget about last night just like she was clearly trying to do.

The interviews at the store and bank where Maria had stopped to get money and food didn't yield any more information. No one remembered her. They'd already seen the security tapes. Jack had been impressed with Bliss's professional demeanor as they'd questioned the store managers and employees. They could pinpoint which employees actually interacted with Maria but unfortunately they had no recollection of her. She'd managed to fade into obscurity. Which was good for Maria but bad for them.

There was a used car lot across from the Wal-Mart where she'd picked up new stuff.

Jack would bet that she'd bought a new car. He didn't think she'd feel comfortable enough on any kind of public transportation, but they couldn't know for sure.

Adams-Larsen had a security watch for her new identity on the booking computer systems for Amtrak and Greyhound. Both he and Bliss thought she'd be too

vulnerable to security cameras and eagle-eyed security. But if she bought a ticket under another name then they were out of luck. It wasn't out of the realm of possibility. Although flying was definitely out of the question.

He had to believe that she would be terrified of Fernandez's reach. After all, the man had kept her locked up for years and no one had ever discovered her.

Once they were airborne, Jack reluctantly headed back to the passenger area.

Jack would have preferred to spend the time hiding in the cockpit with Shane but he needed to go over the information with Bliss and decide on a plan of attack once they landed in Monterey.

He left the cockpit and sat down in the leather seat across the table from Bliss. She had a mug of coffee at her elbow and glasses perched on her nose as she reviewed the papers again.

"We need to come up with a plan once we touch down."

"Okay."

"Since we know Maria won't be able to get to Salinas for another day even if she drives like a bat out of hell, she'll have to stop to sleep, I suggest we pursue the threats Fernandez made."

Bliss nodded. Her red hair gleamed in the bright sunlight pouring in through the oval window. "Sounds good to me. I also want to visit the house where she was held but we need to approach the crime scene carefully." They likely wouldn't be able to squeeze in a visit after they touched down. Even with the time difference, they took off from Iowa around eleven a.m. California time, so when they landed in Monterey there wouldn't be enough daylight to check out Maria's former prison.

Jack agreed. *My, weren't they being civil.* "I want to see the transcript of the cell call. Since this is my backyard, it's possible I'll have a better handle on who and what he's targeting."

Bliss rifled through a beat up black leather delivery bag until she found the paper she was looking for.

Jack scanned the transcript. Fear stabbed him, ice hardened his veins and slowed down his heart.

"What's wrong?"

He hadn't moved and she could tell something was wrong? Jack would dwell on that fact later. Right now he had more pressing problems on his hand.

"This address. It's my office."

"Your company isn't listed at this address," Bliss refuted. "I checked the building occupants myself. We couldn't find any connection between Fernandez and the businesses or tenants."

"GHR and Stone Consulting are actually under the umbrella of JSJ Enterprises. We have the top floor but we're not listed as an occupant. And the building is owned by SAE."

"I know." Bliss crossed her arms over her chest as if getting ready to argue with him. "What does that have to do with you and your company?"

"JSJ is me. Jackson Stone, Junior and SAE stands for Stone Aeronautical Engineering."

"Okay." But recognition was dawning in her gaze, and her eyes narrowed suspiciously. Because everyone had heard of SAE. The company was as ubiquitous to the plane industry as Boeing or Airbus or McDonnell Douglas. "And?"

But he could tell by the way her mouth tightened that she already had a good idea what he was going to say next.

"That's my father."

"So...."

"My family is loaded." He'd never shared that with her. He rarely shared with any of his acquaintances who his father was or the name of his father's company. Bliss had been much more than an acquaintance and he'd never shared intimate details about his family. About his father. About how freaking dysfunctional it all was.

He tried not to have anything to do with dear old dad. Although he wasn't going to deny that the trust fund money he'd inherited at twenty-five had made his life a whole hell of lot easier. And the next installment at thirty-three was how he'd been able to start JSJ Enterprises, Stone Consulting, and Global Humanitarian Relief.

All three of his siblings had pitched in money when they had come on board. But still the bulk of the money had been Jack's. But he'd never told her he was connected to the SAE empire.

"And?"

"And we pay rent and our customers know where we're located but we are not listed as the official occupants. Unless you know us, and we know you, we're...difficult to find."

"I take it that's on purpose."

"Absolutely." Jack bit off. They needed to focus on the real issue here. José Fernandez had singled out his building to watch. That was clear from the transcripts. Fuck.

"And you're upset because—"

"I'm worried about my assistant, Ava." Jack figured that a response to her statement wasn't really necessary. He paced the cabin of the jet. "What if the veiled threat in this transmission was for Ava?"

Bliss stiffened.

Shit. Jack rubbed his hand over the back of his neck

again. They were in midair. They weren't going to land in California for several more hours. He needed to let Connor know he needed to protect Ava. But he had to be discreet.

"It says observe and acquire target." Jack's stomach balled into a knot. Ava had been lucky the day that her friends went missing. She'd stayed home sick from school. Otherwise she might have been abducted too. He knew she lived with that guilt, still. Lived with the haunting question...Why had she been spared?

"I know," Bliss replied. "We're monitoring the police scanners for any unusual activity."

Jack raised his scarred brow. That was pretty slick.

"I told you that I have my brother looking into Fernandez." Jack clarified. "He's using the company computers."

"Your brother works with you?"

Jack let his happiness spread over his face and his mouth curved in a smile. "Yeah. All three of my siblings work for the company now. It took a while but I finally convinced them to come work with me."

Something odd flashed over her face, gone before Jack could decipher what that look meant. Longing?

"That's...nice." Her voice was soft, almost sweet.

"Gives me the chance to look out for everyone."

"Really?"

He knew what she was thinking. When they'd been together, he'd been loose and carefree. But that was after years of taking care of everyone. He shrugged. "They're my responsibility."

"Okay."

And that responsibility spread to his employees as well. "I'm worried about Ava's safety." If the order to observe and acquire was for his brother, Con could take care of himself, but Ava....

"It's slim."

"But if I know about Maria and Ava, it's a very strong possibility that Fernandez does too."

"True."

"I need to call Connor."

"Absolutely not." Bliss didn't say anything else.

Shit. She wasn't going to let him call. Well fuck that. What had happened to the compassionate woman he'd been in love with years ago?

"I need to warn them."

"We can't take the chance that Fernandez has somehow been alerted to the fact that we had a tap on that phone."

"What about the chance that Ava is in danger?"

"Maria is more important that Ava Sanchez." Her face was a cold mask as she shut him down. Her fingers were clenched white around her biceps.

"Seriously?"

"It's for the greater good," Bliss insisted stubbornly.

Fuck. That.

Jack knew from the look on her face, the same look she'd worn when she'd kicked him out years ago that she wasn't going to budge. He couldn't call from the plane anyway, they'd chosen to go unplugged for the corporate jet, so he'd have to wait until they landed.

"Let's focus on what we're going to do once we get to Monterey."

They hammered out a plan, both kept the conversation tight, discussing how they were going to tail Fernandez, and when would be a good time to visit the house where Maria was kept captive. And how they were going to stay away from Jack's office and his siblings.

Jack appreciated her ordered plan and her insight on tracking down Maria. But he had no intention of leaving Con and Ava in the dark.

Hours later they landed in California. Shane brought them down with a smooth as butter landing. As they taxied off the runway and toward their private storage hanger, Jack itched to pull out his phone.

Jack's worry had grown proportionally with every minute they were in the air. He needed to talk to Connor. Wanted to make sure Ava was okay. She was like another sister to him.

While Bliss went to the bathroom, Jack made an executive decision and dialed Connor. "Con?" Jack barked.

"Jack, it really isn't a good time." Con's voice was tense.

Jack could hear sirens and shouting in the background. It sounded like complete chaos.

"Ava is in danger," Jack spit out.

Con said, "Jess, get down here now."

Jess? Jack actually took his phone away from his ear and stared at it for a second.

Con spoke rapidly, "I know. I was trying to fix it."

"I'm worried she's going to be abducted," Jack continued.

"I stopped it."

"Oh, thank God." Jack let a swell of relief roll over him. If Con had taken care of it, everything was good.

"But Jack," Con said. "I'm about to mess up GHR's good name."

Fuck GHR. "Ava's safe?"

"You aren't listening to me. I fucked up and GHR is going to be all over the news."

Jack ignored whatever Con thought he'd done. The most

important issues were Ava and Con's safety. "Ava's okay? You're okay?"

"Yes."

"Thank you, Con, I'm proud of you. You did a good job."

Bliss burst out of the head and ran toward him, a look of pure panic on her face. "Who are you talking to?"

"Shit," Jack blurted out. "Got to run."

Bliss grabbed for his cell phone. "Get off that phone now."

She managed to curl her fingers around his phone and yanked, but since Jack had relayed the message he didn't care.

"You're going to ruin." She jabbed the end button on his cell. "Everything."

He'd protected his family.

Bliss shouted. "Jesus, Jack. Are you trying to send up a spotlight letting Fernandez know we're onto him and that we've lost Maria? And that we're in California?"

"First of all, I didn't mention Maria at all," Jack spoke calmly, quietly. He'd warned his brother and Con was on top of it. That was all he cared about right now. "My brother knows nothing about Maria Torres being found."

Bliss opened her mouth to yell at him again, so he started talking over her objections. "Second, you're making the assumption that Fernandez has our phones tagged."

"Assume everything is tagged." Bliss put her hand to her forehead and paced. "Un-freaking-believable. I should have taken your damn phone away from you."

"I was right. Ava was attacked."

"Bully for you."

Jack hated having to explain himself. He hadn't been

that much of a self-centered ass when they'd been together, had he? He frowned as he tried to make her see reason.

"Look, Bliss," Jack tried to explain. "She's like my little sister. How could I live with myself if something happened to her? I wasn't just blowing off your rules for the hell of it. She's my responsibility."

It was as if he'd punched her. Her shoulders slumped momentarily. And she closed her eyes, blocking the pain reflected in her gaze before she hid it from him.

Bliss's stomach dropped. Damn him.

"My responsibility is Maria." She closed her mouth and breathed hard, trying to control the overwhelming urge to screech at him. How could *he* not understand? Maria was her charge. She'd already lost her once. But she was more than just a job. "I have to protect her at all costs."

"Who *are* you?" Jack shot back. "You have to protect her, even at the expense of my brother and a woman I consider like a sister?"

The blood drained from her face. It was clear from this fight that neither one of them was the person they were thirteen years ago.

"I could ask you the same," she attacked. He'd kept some pretty big things from her. They had practically been living together. Jack had spent most of his nights at her place. It had taken boxes to get all his stuff and clothes from her apartment before he left for the Navy.

Her face had gone from deathly pale to bright red at the memory of his reply to Jill. Her feelings of anger and betrayal simmered and boiled over. "We've met?" she snarled.

"What are you talking about?" Jack tried to play it off. But he knew.

"We've met. That was the sum total of your response

when Jill introduced us?" Her voice stayed even, he would have thought she was calm, except for the sparks shooting from her golden eyes.

Jack was done. The last two days had pushed his patience to the limit and he wasn't the most tactful guy to begin with.

"Yeah, well, what did you want me to say?" Yes, he'd kept things from her but she'd kept things from him as well. He was not the bad guy. So, he'd been trying to protect himself by indicating that their association was casual rather than the truth. "We used to fuck, but then she ripped out my heart?"

Peripherally Jack realized that Shane was standing in the doorway to the cockpit, frozen, clearly trying to be invisible, which was impossible for a six five, black man with a barrel chest and tree trunks for thighs. But Jack gave him points for trying.

Bliss just stared, the bow of her pink lips rounded in a startled O.

"I'll just...take off." Shane's voice rumbled from behind Jack.

And this just turned into a bigger cluster, because Jack was pretty sure they couldn't do this alone. If Bliss didn't want him to contact his brother or Ava, then Jack needed to draft Shane into service.

And fuck but he didn't know if he wanted to continue this conversation with Bliss or pretend he hadn't just left his guts on the sleek, carpeted floor of the Bombardier.

"Sorry, bud." Jack shook his head, his gaze still locked with Bliss's tormented honey eyes. "I know you don't usually do fieldwork but I may need to tap you to do some surveillance."

Bliss's eyebrows rose.

"He's not on the official payroll. He's an independent contractor," Jack said before Bliss could object. "We have him on retainer, but he has other clients as well."

Jack finally broke eye contact and turned to face Shane. "Are you available?"

"Yeah." Shane's voice rumbled deep in his chest. "You had me on call until Thursday, so I blocked out my schedule."

Jack nodded. "Good. Let's get the post flight paperwork out of the way."

"Sure thing."

Jack hesitated, his mouth tight with tension. "Can you grab our stuff and put it in the trunk of Shane's car?"

"Yes," was all she could manage right now.

Jack finished, "And then we can figure out where we're going to stay tonight."

Shane's eyes widened. "You're not going home?"

"Can't, apparently." Jack snarked. "We're worried about some sort of big brother surveillance on me and mine."

Bliss tightened her lips and grabbed her rolling suitcase stowed in the overhead storage above the second grouping of cream leather seats and burled wood tables.

"Okay," Shane said slowly.

"You have enough clothes for the next few days?"

Shane smiled. "Yep."

"What about a weapon?" Jack queried.

"You think I'll need one?" Shane's brows rose. They didn't usually do any work requiring they be armed on U.S. soil. Stone Consulting jobs tended to be in foreign places where maybe the military had trouble operating. Not in the U.S.

"I'd like all of us to be armed."

"Count me in." Shane grinned. "Been awhile since I got to shoot someone."

Jack turned a menacing glare on Shane, his thick black eyebrows lowered into a V above the blade of his nose. "You won't speak of this. It's an extremely sensitive situation."

But it was very clear, he wasn't really talking about the extra work.

CHAPTER 7

Bliss waited in the backseat of Shane's car, a sleek, red Dodge Charger. She couldn't do anything to speed things along. Jack and Shane completed the final shutdown for the plane, threw away their garbage, and closed the private hangar door to secret away the plane.

Jack Stone's private plane. Another trail that Fernandez could trace back to Jack. If Fernandez was monitoring Stone Consulting the plane and their landing was already on his damn radar. She wondered what would happen if they just confronted the jerk. It would certainly get her away from Jack as fast as possible.

But she couldn't do that until she had Maria back in custody.

And she just needed to keep focusing on those details, focusing on how they were going to find Maria, because if she let herself think about the look on Jack's face when he'd revealed how much she'd hurt him, she'd likely start crying. Stupid.

Until last night after her dream, she hadn't cried since her divorce years ago.

But with one sentence that completely came out of left field, he'd reduced her to the emotional mess she'd been after he left.

Yes, *she* had broken up with *him*. But he was already leaving. And she still remembered his stoic face when he'd boxed up his stuff and left for good. She'd cried for days.

Weeks, really.

Once he was done with Basic training all the way in bumfuck Michigan, she'd scoured news reports for any word about soldiers who had fallen. She'd lit candles at the chapel on campus. She'd prayed every day for him to stay safe. Literally for years, she had kept his safety front and center in her mind. Even though she'd been the one to turn him away and she'd done it for her own sanity. She'd still made herself crazy worrying about him.

Bliss clasped her hands in a prayer position and pressed them between her knees.

So how the hell had she ended up here?

Jack and Shane opened their doors, startling Bliss out of her thoughts.

The car shook as they slammed their doors at the same time. She'd keep it completely business. Ignore, ignore, ignore all the personal undercurrents. "Is the plane registered to your company?"

"Yeah. We're out of luck."

Damn.

"But I think I managed to persuade the airport operations manager to 'lose' the landing paperwork for a few days. So hopefully, no one will know we returned until we've got Maria. There's no way to stop the public record from my flight yesterday, which isn't necessarily a bad thing. Assuming Fernandez is keeping track, he'll think I'm out of town."

"Great." An unfamiliar buoyancy filled Bliss. Maybe something was finally going their way.

"Where to?" Shane asked.

Bliss hesitated. The sunlight was gone. "I'd really like to visit the house where she was held. But there are no lights around the house, and the basement electricity was from a generator, so visibility would be nonexistent. It's very isolated."

"First thing tomorrow morning then?" Jack didn't turn around to look at her while he spoke. As a matter of fact he hadn't looked her in the eyes since he'd dropped his bombshell. And she'd circled back to where she didn't want to go.

Their plan was still in place, just postponed. And with Shane as an extra pair of eyes, they'd be able to check out the house quickly in the morning.

"We need to spend the night at a place no one would think Jack Stone would frequent," Bliss said softly. "And someplace where they won't care that we're checking in together."

"Fine. So let's find a place to bunk for the night." Jack gestured to Shane and they were off.

BLISS FUMBLED with the key to the motel room. The aroma of eucalyptus, supposedly a calming scent, nearly overcame the stench of the open dumpster and the ammonia from a fresh urine trail. And this hotel was several steps up from the other places they'd considered. She'd absolutely put her foot down at the sleazy motel with the drug deals going on in the parking lot. Jack hadn't argued and they'd kept looking.

While in the car, they'd turned on the radio and heard the local news. Connor Stone had been the top local story because he'd had a scuffle with Fernandez at his office and the police had been called. So she figured the pressure was on. That information only reinforced her insistence that they stay away from GHR and Stone Consulting. Hopefully, Jack wouldn't try to call his brother again. But still.

They'd finally found this two bedroom suite relatively close to the rural area where Maria had been held and the night manager took cash. She'd eyed Jack speculatively after he requested a room that had access around the back, away from the road. But, she'd finally slapped the old-fashioned key in Jack's hand with a shrug.

Inside the worn hotel suite, the musty scent of mildew from the semi-grungy bathroom lingered in the air. Jack opened the door of the battered, almond-colored refrigerator and shoved the bag of microwave breakfast sandwiches and clamshell of strawberries inside.

"Shane and I will bunk in that room." Jack pointed to the room with two queen beds.

Bliss just gave Shane a long look. "You take the king bed."

"You're kidding?" Jack countered. "Really?"

No way was she giving him the opportunity to call his brother, or even worse, slip out. They were only about thirty miles from Monterey.

Well, this was nothing new. Jack was pissed at her. He was likely to stay that way for a while. And frankly she was still reeling from his blurted admission on the plane.

"I'm hitting the sack." Shane smiled, a wide grin played over his face, a mischievous twinkle in his eyes. "I had a late night last night. What time is reveille?"

"Dawn is at seven a.m." Jack kept his tone to a careful snarl. "Let's be ready to go by six thirty. I want to get this over with."

Bliss couldn't agree more.

The tension between them rose as Shane shut the door to his room and they were alone. Trapped together for the nighttime hours. Which only increased her stress level.

Bliss was already wired. She should be dead on her feet after the last two days. The fact that they couldn't check out the house until tomorrow really chafed. She fought the urge to pace in the tiny living area.

Worry for Maria competed with her feelings about Jack and the last twenty odd hours. It didn't help she kept remembering his intense expressions. Jack's devastated eyes when he'd confessed she'd broken his heart. Jack's head thrown back in ecstasy last night. Jack's stoic face when he'd left thirteen years ago.

It seemed impossible that he had been as destroyed as she had when they'd parted ways so long ago.

A seductive thought twined through her brain. The reason that she'd been afraid years ago was gone. Jack was no longer in the military. No longer putting his life on the line daily. But if she took a chance and it didn't work, she couldn't go through the pain of losing him again.

He pulled the file on Maria out of his duffel.

"You want to go over our plans one more time?" Jack clearly remembered her nearly OCD obsession with details. After her family was torn apart, and when she'd basically become her mother's caregiver, Bliss had developed the need to make sure each and every detail was thought out precisely and nailed down.

It didn't take a shrink to figure out that she needed to be

in command of her life. Because when she'd been younger, everything had been out of her control. When they'd been together, Jack and been content to let her handle everything. He just went along with the flow.

But after working with him for the last twenty-four hours, she'd realized that he was actually almost as anal retentive as she was about controlling details. When had that happened? "I noticed you aren't as laid back as you used to be."

Jack hesitated. "The only time I was ever that relaxed was when I was with you."

"Why?"

Bliss thought for a moment he wouldn't answer. But then Jack said, "That's what happens when you're responsible for your family."

She frowned. "What does that mean?"

Jack was still flipping through the file on Maria. "So you know Marshal Garrett?" Okay, clearly he was changing that subject.

"Not personally." Bliss forced herself to sit. She propped her chin on her palm and rested her elbow on the arm of the faded sofa and studied Jack.

"How did he get Maria from Salinas to DC?"

"Sorry," she said lazily, not sorry in the least. "Trade secret."

Jack raised his brow. The action drew attention to the strip of missing hair. Bliss swallowed and lifted her hand toward his brow. "How'd that happen?"

"Classified," he said abruptly and she dropped her hand back to her lap.

"Looks like we both have secrets," Bliss shot back.

"Yeah. And it's not the first time." Jack cocked his head

and studied her right back. "I guess I didn't know you as well as I'd thought."

"Ditto." Bliss shoved back until she was sitting up, feet on the sofa, knees pressed against her chest as if she could protect her body against his animosity. The anger she'd suppressed earlier came flooding back. "Mr. SAE."

"Don't," Jack said harshly. "SAE is my father. Not me."

His tone was so adamant, Bliss was taken aback. "Well—"

"No. You want to give me a hard time fine. But do not bring up my father."

"Fine. But why didn't you share the information about your family when we lived together?" Bliss's temper started to surface. "I knew you had issues with intimacy, but the fact that you're heir to a billion dollar company should have come up at some time in the year that we were together."

"You really want to go there?" Jack bit out and ignored her assumption that he was next in line for SAE. "What about the fact that you were clearly in some sort of witness protection program? You didn't think that was relevant to share?"

That shut her up.

"I...I'm sorry," she finally said.

"That's it?" Jack threaded his fingers through his hair. "Seriously."

"Not allowed to talk about it, Jack." Bliss wrapped her arms around her calves and rested her cheek on top of her knees. Subconsciously she realized she was making herself as a small a target as possible. Hiding from view. The miniscule amount of InNOut she'd choked down for dinner wasn't sitting well in her stomach. "Fine. Yes. I was in witness protection."

"Was?" He picked up on that little clarification.

"Yeah."

"So the threat is gone?"

"Not exactly." Bliss tried to think about how to give him something without revealing too much.

"Then what exactly?"

"Well, after the initial threat was...eliminated." Tony the Butcher had been killed by a rival mob family while walking out of his house to pick up the morning paper. "I wasn't allowed to go back to my old identity, but they did decide to...transition me out."

Which was a nice way of saying they didn't want to monitor their family any more, at least not the half that included her and her mother. She guessed that had worked out great for her father and sister who were presumably still together somewhere on the West Coast. But for Bliss's mother, that had been the straw that had pushed her over the edge from sad to clinically depressed.

"What about your family?" Jack was eyeing her as if he had figured out that something was really wrong with the scenario she was describing. The tension in her body was hard to miss.

"They had split us up to make us less of a target. My sister and my dad went to one coast and my mom and I went to another."

He was thinking. She could practically see the synapses firing in his brain as he ticked through details at an accelerated pace. "But when we were together you told me your mom committed suicide."

"She did."

"So you're telling me that they wouldn't allow you to go live with the other half of your family?"

"I was eighteen. An adult."

"Who'd been separated from her family for...how many years?" his mouth tightened.

"Four."

"That's utter bullshit."

"Look, Jack. The marshal's system is really designed for criminals who are testifying against their old bosses or associates. The Wit Sec system wasn't set up for people, little kids, who saw things they shouldn't." Her sister had been the only witness to a mob slaying. At first, the authorities thought she'd be safe. But then the mob had blown up her family's house. Luckily, her mom's car had a dead battery at the grocery store and her dad had come to get them. Otherwise the whole family would have gone up in the blast.

"They still shouldn't have left you twisting in the wind after your mom—"

"It was a long time ago. I'm over it." Bliss really wanted off this topic now.

"Jesus, Bliss." Jack straightened. "That's why you used to say that you tried to live up to your name."

Bliss shuddered. She'd been a whole hell of a lot more idealistic back then.

"You chose the name Bliss?"

"Um, yeah." She remembered the moment clearly. She'd been sitting in a nondescript safe house somewhere in Indiana. She'd just said goodbye to her father and sister. At the time she hadn't known that she was saying goodbye for the last time. The entire situation was supposed to be temporary.

So, being the idealistic, cheerful teen that she was she'd cut out inspirational slogans and taped them on her bedroom walls and vowed to be happy until it was all over.

An adventure her dad had called it.

The fun never ends. She suppressed the need to shed tears. It was a long time ago. She was over it. And even if she wasn't, crying about it wouldn't change anything.

As if he couldn't help himself, Jack threw himself down next to her and curled his arm around her shoulders, pulling her tight into his embrace. "God damn, I'd like a few minutes alone in a room with the bureaucrat who decided it was expedient to keep you apart."

Bliss held herself stiffly in his arms afraid to relax. Afraid to let down her guard. So when he realized he was embracing her, and he moved away she would still be composed. *Hold it together just a few more minutes.*

She'd forgotten that need to grasp onto every day with purpose. To make each experience one to remember. Lost in the daily grind of life and just surviving one day at a time.

"So that's why you do what you do?" Jack said against her hair, "Help other people the way you wished you'd been helped?"

"Adams-Larsen makes regular people disappear," Bliss confessed. It wasn't exactly against policy. Jill had given Bliss leeway to explain to Jack what they do. Her stomach curdled. Jill had actually wanted Bliss to talk up the agency.

She thought Jill might be setting the groundwork for Adams-Larsen to do some joint work with Jack's company but Jill hadn't given her the specifics of what she had in mind.

"That's your job?" He asked as if he needed to clarify one more time.

"Yes." She nodded against his shoulder. The heat from his body sent tendrils of warmth curling through her. "Obviously there has to be some sort of extenuating circumstance. A whistleblower, avoiding an abusive ex or not so ex, even civilians who testify against criminals sometimes.”

“Damn, Bliss.”

“It’s a good thing.”

“You would know better than most.” Jack continued to pet her, stroking her back through the thin boring white cotton shirt, rubbing her shoulders as if he could soothe away the hurts of her past.

But she could tell he was processing too, when he asked suddenly, “What made you send me away?”

That empty place inside that had been growing within Bliss since she saw him again widened. She really didn’t want to get into this. Didn’t want him to know how messed up she’d really been. But, after his confession earlier today, she owed him.

“It would be nice to hear the truth.” His request was issued softly, as if he didn’t want to jar her, but there was grit layered beneath his easy tone and gentle hands.

“I was terrified,” she told his collarbone, her cheek pressed against his pecs and the soft material of his plain black t-shirt. And she decided that honesty couldn’t hurt either of them now.

He stilled at her harsh words. “Of what?”

“That you would die.”

“So you shoved me out the door?” Jack’s hold loosened on her shoulders. “Frankly I’m not seeing the logic.”

“It wasn’t logical. It was emotional. You were already leaving,” Bliss replied. “I couldn’t handle the fact that you’d be in danger. I lived with that fear for my family for four years. I couldn’t see any way out.” Her throat constricted.

“God...damn.”

“I’m sorry.” And a single tear slid down her cheek. She

was sorry. But she'd suffered for the choice too. She didn't know if that would make him happy or not.

"Don't cry." Jack cupped her cheek in his palm and rubbed at the single trail with his rough thumb.

The room seemed to heat as the air around them shrunk until Bliss only saw Jack. Only felt Jack. He seemed larger than life and so very solid. Here was the Jack who she'd fallen in love with the first time.

His bicep was hard around her shoulders, and she was wrapped in safety. She looked up into his stippled hazel eyes, mesmerized by the tenderness and compassion shimmering in them.

He asked softly, "What happened to living every day with bliss?"

She'd been so stupidly idealistic. She blushed, licked her lips. Jack's gaze zoomed to the swipe of her tongue and he groaned. "Bliss."

He tilted her chin up and met her mouth with his. The first brush of his lips was tender, fraught with apology and the need to give her some affection. The stubble from his ten o'clock shadow rasped against her softer skin.

Bliss inhaled his hot scent. The hint of his shaving cream, evergreen from his deodorant, and the musk that was all Jack. He still smelled the same. Like Jack. Like love.

She knew that was wrong, but she couldn't help but respond to the memories.

Bliss feathered light kisses across his jaw as he curved his arm around her waist, lifted her across his lap, and held her tight against his solid mass. His erection prodded her hip as he bowed over and captured her mouth with his.

That quickly, tenderness was replaced by a burning passion.

Jack skimmed his hands along the curve of her waist.

She was more woman than girl now, curvy in all the right places. He scooped her ass in his hands and lifted her so she straddled his lap and his raging erection.

They had always been like this. Combustible.

Jack forced himself to slow down. This time he was taking it slow. And yeah, sex with Bliss was probably a mistake. But in this moment, he didn't care.

Bliss's arms clung to his neck and she held on as if she'd never let go.

Jack slid his fingers beneath another bland, manly cotton button up shirt and explored the familiar softness of her skin. She was supple and smooth beneath his rougher fingertips. He brushed his thumbs back and forth along her ribs, easing the material up in slow motion, each swipe brought his fingers that much closer to her breasts.

Jack lifted her up onto her knees and pressed a hot kiss against her belly button. Bliss's stomach contracted at the intimate swirl of his tongue. He dragged his tongue up the center of her body even as his palms finally cupped her perfect globes. He nipped at each rib, following the path of his hands, while he lazily rubbed her hardened nipples.

A scented heat wafted from her skin, jasmine mingled with the musk of her arousal.

His cock throbbed as she surrendered to his sensual raid. Her fingers threaded through his hair and rubbed his scalp and neck as she anchored him closer to her.

"God, Jack," she whimpered as he suckled one hard lace-covered nipple into his mouth. Even her underwear had been washed of color, the nude lace was feminine but lacked the vibrancy that had once been Bliss's trademark.

Her knees dipped as he continued to suck and lick her nipples. Jack turned and pushed her back onto the seat of the sofa, and she sank down into the cushions.

Bliss was busy trying to rip his t-shirt over his head. He released her breasts long enough to grab the shirt from behind his neck in one fist and yank it off.

Bliss ran her hands over his bunched biceps and down his arms until she could pull him further over her body. Jack was on his knees between her spread thighs. She pulled him closer until their mouths connected again.

Bliss rubbed her tongue into his mouth. And fuck him, but all the blood rushed to his cock. *Slow, slow.* He repeated the words like a mantra, even as his hands were busy unbuttoning her shirt.

Jack opened to her kiss as she wrapped her legs around his waist and rubbed the heat of her sex against his bare abs. Damn, she was like an inferno. And the temptation to rip off her pants and pound into her was like a fever in his blood.

He eased his mouth away from hers, even as she curled her legs tighter and rocked into him.

He needed to savor. He needed to tell her with his body what he couldn't say with words. Jack spread the shirt open, baring her lace-covered breasts, and stomach to his gaze. Jack pressed a line of kisses across her collarbone like a necklace and then suckled the hollow in her neck.

"Dammit, I missed you," she groaned out as he slowly unbuttoned her black suit pants. The sleek material showed off her high, tight ass to perfection. The zipper was loud over the labored sound of their breathing.

Jack rubbed his thumbs in the crease between her thigh and hip, each lazy swipe took him closer to the ridge of her pubis and she lifted her hips seeking his touch. Instead he ran his hands over her legs and behind his back to her ankles, gently unhooking them from his body.

Bliss let her legs fall apart, the hint of nude lace panties was revealed in the open v of her pants, and her body was splayed in wanton surrender. Jack took a moment to admire her, lips puffy from their kisses, skin slightly pink from the scrape of his beard across her chest and belly, the tips of her nipples poking through the delicate lace of her bra. She was undone.

All for him.

With one smooth move, he slid her pants and panties down her legs and off, tossing them onto the coffee table next to him.

Paradise waited between her thighs and before she could object, Jack dove into her. He lifted her legs until her thighs were over his shoulders, ran his hands down her legs then pressed his palms against the tender curve of her belly. She was completely exposed to him and in his control. The move lifted her ass slightly, and finally Jack bent to her sex.

He rubbed his nose against her clit and then smiled at her little 'oh' of surprise. Jack kissed the swollen button pushing out of the nest of auburn curls. Then with little fanfare he began to eat at her in earnest. He flattened his tongue and licked her opening from the bottom of her lips to her clit, over and over again. With each lick he curled just a little more into her until his mouth was pressed tight against her sex, his tongue was fucking her and his stubble abraded her clit. She was rocking her hips and sex against his mouth so hard, he knew she was close. Jack pressed on her belly and gobbled her up.

Bliss's fingers tightened in his hair. Little whimpers escaped as she bowed up jamming her sex against his mouth even as her womb contracted against the press of his palms and she flew apart. With every moan and sigh, his cock pulsed against the constraint of his zipper.

How could he have let this go? He should have pushed

harder. Demanded answers when they'd been younger. Instead he'd dragged his wounded, destroyed heart to Basic and wallowed in misery.

But he was here now and she was opening to him. He'd be a fool if he didn't seize this opportunity.

Bliss was blind, deaf, dumb, her entire body engaged in the intense pleasure that caromed throughout her. Jack was pressing sweet soft kisses against her inner thighs, his fingers stroking the sensitive skin of her belly, trying to bring her down from the mind blowing high of release.

A shiver worked over her body as she rubbed her foot against the hot hard length of him. His erection was trapped in the confines of his cargo pants. Bliss wasn't about to let that erection go to waste.

She reached between their bodies and tugged on the waist of Jack's pants. "Off. Now."

Jack smiled against her belly. He kissed the same path up her body, taking his time, suckling each breast with slow lazy draws. Jack's heart bulleted in his chest, thrilled with the urgency of her actions as she shoved his pants to his knees.

He managed to maintain a leisurely exploration of her skin and body until she curled her palm around his erection.

His hips surged into her hand as she squeezed with the perfect amount of pressure then rubbed her thumb over the weeping tip. Jack groaned. "Jesus, Bliss."

She was everywhere. Her feet were pushing his pants down his legs, even as her hand guided him to her slick core. His bare cock rubbed against her swollen aroused flesh. Bliss's breath caught as he nudged her entrance. The proof of her completion coated the tip of his cock and he slipped inside her.

And oh, my God, he slid inside her like he'd never left.

Her sex swallowed him up and enveloped him in a sheath of love and perfection.

He was full to bursting. Full of urgency to claim her. Full of the need to be with her again. Full of an emotion he refused to name. To have her take him in and accept him in without reservation.

Jack shuddered at the slick velvet clasp that surrounded his cock. Each slow foray in, his head rubbed over the swollen ridge of her g-spot. He wanted to get lost in the sensation of her body. The soft pillow of her breasts, the sharp points of her nipples against his pecs, the sweet cradle of her hips, and the sweet dig of her heels into his ass.

He re-learned her body with this slow exploration, his balls snugged up against her swollen sex, as he pulsed in small movements, filling her up, and her sex welcomed him with a heated embrace.

Jack was propped up on his elbows, their lower bodies pressed together. He brushed a lock of hair from her damp cheek and stared into her dazed honey eyes.

She was lost in the grip of her pleasure.

A feeling of extreme triumph roared through him. He had done that to her. Jack pressed a kiss against her lips, and increased his pace, pulling out until only the tip of his cock brushed her clit and then powering back inside. Bliss's hips rose to meet each thrust, her body responding again to his intimate foray, until each time Jack was buried to the hilt. Her sex tightened around his cock until she arched and groaned.

Her orgasm milked his cock and shot him over the edge. Jack surged inside her, his cock gripped by the rhythmic pulse of her contractions. Each sexual squeeze caressed him, and his orgasm began at the base of his spine and then burst through him in a kaleidoscope of pleasure.

Nothing had ever been sweeter than sex with Bliss and it seemed that in thirteen years, that hadn't changed.

He ached for all the things they'd lost, for all the time they'd lost. But he was smart enough to understand that if he shared that with her, she would close up, close off. Instead he would give her pleasure, and take his own. They had to get through this situation with Maria and then they could see where this might lead.

CHAPTER 8

She and Jack were ignoring the fact that they'd had sex, again, last night.

It had been amazing and made her long for the chance to deepen the connection that had had seemed to tentatively grow between them, like a tiny sliver of light that with time could strengthen into a true, strong beam.

But when they'd woken up this morning, the walls were back in place and right now the last thing they needed to focus on was their relationship. Or whatever it was.

Jack and Shane were in the front seat of the Charger with Bliss in the back, and they were on their way to the place where Maria had been held for eight long years.

Bliss knew the house would be difficult for her to see. Emotionally she related to Maria's situation. The girl had been torn away from everything she'd known in a heartbeat and thrust into a situation where she had no control and no way out. Instead of giving up and resigning herself to the fate of a victim and a captive, Maria had spent painstaking years digging her way out of her prison.

In a lot of ways, Bliss had been lucky. Once she turned

eighteen, she'd had options. She'd been able to make her own choices. And she had chosen her life. Chosen her path and thrown off the mantle of suppression of the witness protection program. They may have cut her loose but she owned it, and she embraced the fact that she was free. Even if she hadn't been able to ever see her father and sister again. And felt that lack still. She'd been able to make her own choices, unlike Maria.

Her heart thudded in her chest. The boom-boom echoed in her ears made it hard to hear the murmured conversation in the front seat. The powerful V8 engine rumbled beneath her as Shane punched the gas and they headed toward the house where Maria was held captive.

Bliss swallowed down bile. She'd seen the crime scene pictures. The marshal's office had sent in techs to document everything right away. The pictures had been overnighted to her as none of the information was in the marshal's computer system.

They had concluded immediately that all information about Maria needed to stay old school. Paper only. No cyber trail that could be followed and jeopardize Maria Torres's safety.

Twenty minutes or so after leaving their hotel, they were bumping along a cracked and neglected route. The two lane road was lined with overgrown brambles and trees whose branches met in an arch over the road, trimmed to allow trucks and other vehicles through. The branches had grown together creating a tunnel that blocked out the sunrise. The high beams from the Charger cut through the dark warren-like atmosphere and illuminated the eerie road.

"The entrance is coming up on the right," Bliss said tensely from the backseat.

"We should go past the drive and continue on," Jack directed.

"There isn't much else out here." Bliss gripped the back of the headrest. She'd reviewed the topography maps thoroughly. "And nothing past this entrance. The last 'property' on the road literally fell down about twenty years ago. Maria traveled through two canyons to get to Marshal Garrett's property." More of her luck. It really was incredible.

"What are the odds that Fernandez has it under surveillance?"

"None." Bliss's anxiety ramped up to a new level. "He and whoever was bringing Maria supplies need to stay as far away from this property as possible."

"There could be cameras," Jack argued, while Shane navigated the increasingly bumpy drive.

"There was no evidence of cameras when the crime scene techs did their investigation of the property."

A dip in the landscape led down to a creek that ran alongside the barren road.

"Jesus, she escaped through this?" Jack muttered as they drove into a small clearing. The tiny house, little more than a living room, kitchen, bath and bedroom, backed up to the creek. It was barely a thousand square feet and had clearly been built over a hundred years ago. A porch ran the width of the house and two rickety steps lead to the front door.

Once upon a time this had been a homestead. Overgrown roses bordered the porch, some blooms clung desperately to their petals. There was rusted tilling equipment off to the side and tattered curtains hung in the cracked and rippled glass of the windows.

"Shane, keep watch while we check it out," Jack commanded.

"You got it, boss."

Fog swirled in the early morning. Dawn was barely more than a pink-edged sky. Squirrels clicked and chattered as they scampered up the thick eucalyptus trunks. The birds were silent. The creek bed was dry. Small rodents rustled in the underbrush. Smells battled for dominance, the piney scent of eucalyptus, the decay of underbrush and leaves, and the faded sweet of the porch roses. Besides the animals, the quiet was absolute.

"Who owns the house?" Jack asked gruffly as they approached the front porch.

"It appears to be abandoned." Bliss shifted into business mode. "In theory it was foreclosed on about ten years ago. The previous owners left."

"Can they be tied back to Fernandez in any way?"

Bliss shook her head, even though he wasn't looking at her. "So far we've been unable to find a connection."

"Then why hasn't the bank taken possession?"

"That's where it gets a little murky." Bliss huffed out a breath. "According to county records it was foreclosed on by Banke of America."

"So why not go back to Bank of America?"

"Because it's B-A-N-K-E of America." Bliss continued, "On the surface it looks like a typo. But the real B of A has no record of foreclosing on the property."

"Have you thought about seeing if there are any other properties registered to the company with that typo?" Jack mulled over the discrepancy.

"We have a forensic accountant working on it."

"I could ask Connor."

"Not necessary." Bliss shut him down before he could offer to call his brother again.

Jack said, "I would think you'd want everyone working

on this, if we can tie the house back to Fernandez, it is one more piece of evidence."

He was right but..."We can't risk that he's monitoring your brother and Ava after yesterday."

Bliss knew she was right. But she understood his wish to figure this out and to use the resources he had at his disposal.

They breeched the porch at the same time.

Bliss wondered if they'd have to break down the door, but as she approached she noted the handle was broken, the knob crooked in its bore hole, and the door held shut with a single strand of twisted metal wire.

Bliss uncoiled the wire and stepped into the darkened, nearly empty house. In the living room, an old sofa had been nibbled on by rodents and rested on a rug worn bare in spots, and a single chair sat in the kitchen. Bliss swallowed and searched for the entrance to the basement. A fine powder dusted all the surfaces where someone might have left fingerprints. The handles and faucet in the sink, the sashes, the locks of the fragile windows, the door knobs. It took all of two minutes to determine there were no stairs to the basement.

Jack lifted the rug and there, almost invisible in the rough plank floor, was a trap door. "In the ground."

She'd told him. But he hadn't really heard her.

There had to be a trick to finding the way to lift the door. Bliss ran her fingers along the seam of the door, looking for any way to lift it. At the very edge was a hinged piece, and when she pushed, the small piece folded in and Bliss was able to curl her fingers around the edge and lift.

She pulled up the trap door and flipped it until it lay flat on the floor. Inside was another smaller door with a cat door installed in the center. Both doors were dusted with the fingerprint powder. The larger trap door had been welded to the floor support beams. The welding had been cut for the crime techs to get down into the basement and search for any evidence against her jailors, but they'd found nothing that wasn't directly attributable to Maria.

Bliss pulled a pair of vinyl gloves from her messenger bag and snapped them on her hands quickly before continuing. They had both taken out their flashlights.

Inset in the metal door was the pet door, designed for a cat or a very small dog, on hinges to push inward. So her captors could literally just drop bags of food and supplies in. The flap was fitted with a spring mechanism so that it snapped closed as soon as the pressure from above was off. The way the door was installed would have made it impossible for Maria to get out. All the mechanisms were on the outside of her prison.

Bliss pushed the cat door open and shined her flashlight on the small room. A twin bed was in the corner, an exercise bike in another corner, a mini-fridge and a hot pad sat on a Formica counter, and a television perched on a wood plank resting over two cinder blocks.

That was it.

Black powder covered every surface.

"Jesus," Jack muttered from beside her. She'd been doing her best to ignore how close he was but as his breath feathered over the back of her neck, Bliss was forced to acknowledge the sweet warmth emanating from his body, and his solid comforting bulk beside her.

"No stairs?" Jack whispered.

"They dropped her food down once a week and she gave them her garbage. All the fingerprints they found down there were hers." Bliss revealed softly, "I don't think they ever went down into the hole once they sealed it off."

"How," Jack swallowed. "How the hell did she escape?"

"She saw Shawshank Redemption. She used the handles of a plastic spoons until they broke. She basically dug a tunnel out to the creek. You can't see the walls but they are papered with posters of woods."

Jack's forehead dropped to her shoulder. "I'm sorry."

That was unexpected. "What for?"

"I understand." Jack's lips moved against the bare skin of her neck. "I still need to protect my family but I get why you don't want anything else to jeopardize her safety."

Bliss shivered at the heat of his body pressed up against hers. His casual touch set off tremors inside her. If he didn't move soon, she was going to start shaking on the outside.

"Guys," Shane called softly. "You need to get out. Now."

The urgency in Shane's voice galvanized Jack. He pushed to standing on his powerful thighs and pulled her up with him.

"What are you doing?"

"Shane is the most even keeled guy I know. If he sounds that panicked then we need to listen."

He didn't sound panicked to her. As Bliss stood, the arc of light from her flashlight scanned the basement prison and something caught her eye. Holy shit. "Jack. We can't leave yet."

"Bliss, we have to go." Jack pulled on her arm.

"Maria," Bliss shouted. "It's Bliss Lee. Will you come out?"

"What?" Jack hissed.

"Guys, we really need to get out of here." Shane's voice lifted. "Like five minutes ago."

"Maria, you're in danger here." But that flash of fabric, the pattern on one of the dresses that Bliss had given Maria, was gone.

Fuck.

"Are you sure you saw something?" Jack's palm curled around her bicep.

Bliss whirled, her face inches from Jack's. "I am not leaving her behind. She's down there, Jack."

"Okay. I believe you." His hand on her shoulder was soft, placating.

"Maria, honey, come on out." Bliss tried to keep her tone from being too desperate but at Jack's look, she knew she hadn't succeeded.

"Maria, my name is Jack Stone. Your friend Ava Sanchez would really like to see you."

They both heard the rustling at the same time. Bliss averted her light from the open hole so that it wouldn't shine in Maria's face.

"Maria, it's not safe here." Bliss gave up and begged, "Please, please, come out. *Por favor.*"

Jack said, "You remember Ava. She never forgot you. Never."

Suddenly, Maria's pale, gaunt face appeared in the opening. She was wearing the dress that had been captured on the security cameras and tears tracked down her cheeks. "Ava?"

"Yeah. I know she would love to see you." Jack knelt down and lowered his arm into the opening. "Grab hold and I'll get you out of there."

Maria clambered up on a chair and reached up to Jack.

Dawn had broken, the sun was mostly obscured by the gray marine layer fog, and with the tangle of tree canopy, only random streaks of pink rippled in the early morning sky. It was still pretty dark, which was a good thing. Otherwise, Bliss wasn't sure they could have gotten Maria to leave the basement.

Once Jack pulled her up into the living room, Bliss curled her arm around Maria's shaking shoulders. Bliss was pretty sure she was shaking too. "I'm so glad to see you."

"Hurry, guys," Shane called out.

Maria stiffened.

"It's okay. He's with us." Bliss reassured Maria as Jack asked, "What's wrong?"

They were out the door and Bliss still couldn't see any threat. But she thought she heard a cell phone ringing in the distance.

"We need to get the hell out of here." Shane was running toward the car.

The smell of gasoline suddenly hit Jack's nose and he could hear the muffled ring tone of a cell phone.

"Fuck. Is that what I think?" Jack started running toward the car, shoving Bliss and Maria in front of him as Shane threw himself into the drivers' seat and the engine roared to life.

Shane answered, "Remote detonator. With this brush, the entire canyon is going to go up in a few seconds."

"Can we stop it?" Bliss asked.

"I don't know where the phone is, based on the echo of sound, it's somewhere in the brush by the creek," Shane said calmly as he yanked the wheel into a sharp U turn.

"Shouldn't we go look for it?"

"No time." Jack shook his head. "Because of how dry our fall and winter has been, once it catches the entire place is going ignite. If we don't get out now, *we* won't make it. Forget about the house, with all this tinder, it's going to be an inferno."

CHAPTER 9

Shane gunned the engine and the Charger leapt forward, bouncing on the uneven path back to the main road.

"We have to call Garrett." But Bliss didn't have any hands. Maria was clinging tight to her fingers. Oh my God. She'd been right!

Elation filled her. She'd been right. She'd found Maria.

But that elation was tempered by the devastation they were leaving behind. The house ignited in a whoosh.

Bliss craned her neck, staring out the back of the car window as the house was instantly engulfed in flames. The blaze reminded her of her own childhood home. Destroyed by fire and ultimately what lead to their family's separation. They'd been lucky they hadn't been home.

Maria had been lucky that Bliss, Jack, and Shane were there.

What if she hadn't thought this is where Maria would go? What if they hadn't gotten here in time? What if they'd set the house on fire last night? She would have never forgiven herself.

"We have to call this in," Jack said. "With the current drought, this fire could spread fast."

Shane was busy calling 9-1-1 on his cell but it was going to be far too late. The entire house would be a smoldering pile of ash before the local fire trucks made it to the ignition point.

With one trembling hand, Bliss dialed Marshal Garrett's cell. Bliss hoped that the retired marshal answered since she was using a burner phone they'd picked up last night. She spoke urgently to him as thankfully he answered his phone. "Someone torched the house. We already called emergency services but you may need to evacuate. Dammit, I'm sorry, Garrett."

Her stomach roiled as she realized that another piece of evidence against Fernandez had just been eliminated. It didn't matter that the way it disappeared was extremely suspicious. Without the house and the trace evidence of Maria's captivity, Fernandez eliminated another link to him. Even though they had crime scene pictures, the destruction of the property was a blow.

Marshal Garrett was still speaking in her ear. "Thank goodness we got the techs there before it went."

Maria clung to Bliss, shivering, likely in shock. "Sorry, Garrett. I've got to go." She didn't want him to know that she had Maria right next to her, not safely tucked away somewhere else in the country after he took the initiative to get her to DC.

But Garrett wasn't finished. "We've got to wait until we get the DNA results back. We should have them tomorrow. But we can't make a move until we have definitive proof that she is Maria."

Bliss knew that. But now that they had Maria in custody

again, Bliss was antsy to get the confrontation with Fernandez out of the way. "Let me know as soon as you've got the results. You can call me on this phone." And she disconnected the call.

Dammit.

"Do you think they knew we were there?" Bliss asked Jack and Shane the question that was weighing on her mind. They hadn't seen any evidence of surveillance cameras and the crime scene techs from the marshal's office hadn't found any but what were the odds?

"I think my brother spooked Fernandez. The groundwork was likely already laid so that they could torch the house as soon as it looked like they needed to. They probably set it up as soon as they discovered she was missing."

Which would have been only three days ago. After the crime scene techs were done.

Shane said, "I didn't even smell the gasoline until I decided to check the back of the house. The ground was saturated. I think it was dumb luck—"

"Or something," Jack muttered.

"—that we were there when they set it off." Shane sped down the dirt lane, his gaze cutting to the fireball that rose behind them.

Bliss flinched as an explosion boomed behind them. She felt as if this whole operation was cursed. She thunked her forehead on the headrest behind Shane.

With her right hand, she held on to Maria.

"Where to?" Shane asked.

"We need to get back to our hotel," Bliss directed him. "And get Maria hidden."

There was no way she could let Maria out of her sight.

It was imperative that Fernandez not get a lock on Maria's location.

"Well, boss, where to?" Shane asked Jack again.

Bliss fumed. Really?

"You heard the lady," Jack deferred to Bliss. "Back to the hotel."

Bliss relaxed.

"And then we're calling in backup," Jack said in a firm tone.

As much as she wanted to argue, he was right. They had their witness. But before they could set up the confrontation that would bury Fernandez, they had to get all the evidence and their ducks in a row. And Bliss was going to need help guarding Maria.

They needed to make sure Maria didn't bolt, again.

"You need to talk to us, honey." Jack's voice was unbelievably gentle as he stared at Maria.

"At the hotel," Bliss interjected.

"Okay," Jack agreed. And then he brought up back up again.

While they drove back to the hotel, they argued about who they were going to call as backup. Shane navigated the back roads, and watched Bliss and Jack hash out who they were going to call for help like it was a match at Wimbledon.

Bliss wanted Marshal Garrett. Maria was comfortable around Garrett.

Jack wanted Connor and Ava.

The worst part of arguing with Jack was she saw his point, she just didn't think it was safe. She could tell by the way Maria reacted when Jack told Maria that Ava remembered her, that seeing Ava Sanchez would be a good thing.

But the fact remained that they couldn't call them. "We can't have Ava Sanchez or your brother anywhere near Maria until we can go public. Fernandez has to be totally spooked by what your brother and Ava did yesterday. So he's getting rid of evidence. And he's got to know now that the house is a dead end. We want him to relax, not get more stressed."

As their conversation escalated, Maria interrupted. "No Ava."

That shut them both up. "Why not?" Jack asked.

"I don't want her in any danger." And with that plea, Maria sealed Bliss's argument. But the fact remained that they needed help.

Jack snapped his fingers. "Keisha."

"Who?"

"She works for GHR."

"Great, Jack. A relief worker?"

"She's got...other skills."

"Um, Jack." Shane tried to interrupt.

"Not now, Shane."

"But—"

"We're good." Jack cut Shane off. But Bliss had had enough.

"I'm curious what Shane has to say." Bliss balled her fists and put her hands on her hips. "Please continue, Shane."

"She's a scary woman."

Shane, the giant badass, thought this Keisha was scary? That didn't sound good.

But Jack dismissed Shane's words with a flick of his hand. "She can be. She can also be a total marshmallow."

"We talking about the same woman?" Shane's eyebrows rose along with his voice. "She's a total ball buster."

Jack snorted. "Keisha is perfect. She can guard Maria and keep her safe."

"How are we going to get here?"

"Easy." Jack bared his teeth. "Shane is going to call and invite her over."

CHAPTER 10

Shane called from the car and arranged for Keisha to meet him at the hotel. By tacit agreement, he didn't mention Jack at all. They had been back in their room less than five minutes when there was a decisive knock at the door.

Shane peered out the security peephole in the door. "It's her. I just want to reiterate, she is going to be *pissed*."

Another loud bang on the door had Shane jumping back. "Shit."

Jack watched Bliss stifle a laugh. It startled him. It was the first genuine smile he'd seen on her face since they reconnected.

Shane yanked open the door. "Hey, Keisha. Come on in."

"Oh, hell no, I want answers first," Keisha shot back. "What's this about?"

"We really need privacy." Shane pulled her into the room.

"What is wrong with you?" Even though she was a foot shorter, she twisted to break his hold, jabbed him in the stomach, and was reaching for the doorknob when Jack stepped into her view.

"Hey, Keish." Jack smiled broadly. She had been one of his absolute best hires. Keisha Johnson had attitude in spades. She topped out at five foot five but her personality was so big, he never noticed how short she really was. She had tight, dark brown curls with streaks of gold. Her skin and hair always seemed to shimmer with bronze. Even better, she was a killer logistics manager but wasn't afraid to get her hands dirty. And while she did have a bit of a chip on her shoulder, she also had a soft center that most people never noticed.

Shane slammed the door shut with an oof. For an infinitesimal moment, some raw emotion flashed in Keisha's eyes. Disappointment. Hurt. What? Hell if he knew, but he did understand that somehow, something had just hurt her.

"Jack?" Keisha noticed Maria on the sofa, and Bliss standing behind her with a soft expression on her face. "I thought we were supposed to be on vacation."

"Yeah. You are. But I needed you," Jack said with a shrug of his shoulders.

Shane rubbed his large hand over his abs. "Sorry for the subterfuge."

"What's going on?" Keisha demanded answers, her attitude firmly in place, chin up and curls shaking, as she looked at the two women. "Who are the two chicks?"

Bliss held out her palm and introduced herself. Keisha scanned her, raised an eyebrow at the suit, and then shifted her attention to Maria. Bliss put a protective hand on Maria's shoulder. "This is Maria Torres."

Shane had faded into the background. But if Jack was right, Keisha seemed to be consciously avoiding looking in that corner of the room.

"Why does that name sound familiar?" Keisha split her focus between Jack and Maria.

"She's one of the girls who were abducted eight years ago."

"Hol-ee shit. Is this why Connor and Ava were accused of harassing—"

"Kind of. But you can't say anything to anyone." Jack cautioned. "They don't know she's alive yet."

Keisha's head snapped toward Maria so fast her curls hit her in the face. She was moving before Jack could say another word. Keisha threw herself down on the sofa. "It's a fricking miracle." She lifted her hand as if she was going to stroke Maria's hair then paused. "Okay if touch you, baby?"

Maria nodded.

"You're a survivor." Keisha wrapped her arms around Maria and hugged her tight. "Don't you forget it."

Shane's jaw dropped. Jack's heart swelled. He'd been right. Keisha was perfect.

Maria seemed to just crumple in Keisha's arms. She dropped her head to Keisha's shoulder and began to cry silently.

Bliss had wrapped both arms around her waist and was watching the scene play out between Maria and Keisha with pure distress. Jack wanted to hug her tight too. She was shaking and he could tell that Maria's acceptance of the physical comfort had shocked her. And she was beating herself up over not anticipating what Maria needed.

"So what do you need from me?" Keisha pulled out her smart phone and sat poised, body tense and fierce, even as she kept one arm loosely wrapped around Maria's shoulders. Jack knew he could ask her to take someone out right now and her only question would be: soft or hard?

"Damn. I knew you'd be perfect." He chose great

employees. "We need you to protect Maria. So we can go after the man who did this."

Her hazel eyes sparkled with determination. "On it."

"And we need to get her clothes for the press conference."

Maria stiffened.

Keisha bent and murmured in her ear. "You gotta do it. I know it's goin' to be hard but he needs to *pay*."

"Bliss and I will set up the logistics. Your job is to take care of our guest."

"You don't need to worry about a thing." Keisha smiled at Maria, everything about her radiated peace and determination.

Shane was still propped up against the wall, his gaze glued to Keisha as if he'd never seen her before.

Jack could understand. He and Keisha had met during Basic at the Great Lakes Naval Training Center. He'd only seen the surface of Keisha for years until they'd happened to work together and he'd seen the sweet beneath her gruff. "Maria. We let you have your time. But now we need to know everything you told the marshals. We need every single detail you can remember so that he doesn't get away with what he did."

Keisha said, "You need to tell us all about it."

Maria began in a halting monologue. Her voice was like sandpaper on rough wood. Jack realized she'd likely not spoken much in the last eight years.

She spoke for hours. She told them about the abduction. How scared the four girls had been. About how Fernandez had taken one look at Maria and freaked. "Why did you take her? It was only supposed to be the three."

Jack broke out into a sweat when Maria admitted that

normally she walked to the fields with Ava. She shot him a beseeching look.

"I promise you that you will see Ava tomorrow. We need to make sure she stays safe."

It was as if he said the magic words. Maria's whole body relaxed, she nodded her short chin length hair bobbed against her neck. "We must keep Ava safe."

Jack's heart swelled at the thought of Ava reuniting with Maria again. He couldn't wait to make that happen.

"So you were a mistake?" Bliss spoke evenly.

"Yes." Maria smiled sadly. "But the other three, apparently they were dispensable."

"What happened to them?" Jack asked softly.

Maria started shaking again. "The two men, they came to take them away."

Jack stiffened. This was going to be bad.

"Sofia, she was a virgin and the one…he hurt her." Maria started to cry again.

"Bastard," Keisha whispered.

"*Dios mio*, the blood it was everywhere." Maria wiped the tears from her face with trembling fingers. "And then she didn't move."

One of the captors had raped her. It sounded like she'd hemorrhaged to death. Fuck. Jack wanted to rage and shout but that wouldn't help Maria right now. "Do you know what they did with her?"

"They buried her in the forest."

"Which one?" Jack's brain was working at hyper speed. If they could find Sofia's body, it would be one more nail in Fernandez's coffin.

"Point Lobos."

That was on the coast, but there was the meadow. Jack thought about the Lace Lichen Trail. With the moss and shadowy, muted light, it would be the perfect place to hide a body. They might never find her.

Bliss asked softly, "What about the other two girls?"

Maria pursed her mouth. "I never saw them again."

"And you only saw Fernandez one time?"

"Yes."

"But you're sure it was him?"

"*Si*. Yes. He was a friend," she spat the word. "Of my parents."

That must be why Fernandez was so upset when they'd grabbed Maria.

Jack had one last question for her. He knew it would hurt. And he hated to have to ask. Dammit.

But Keisha beat him to it. "Why'd he leave you in that hole, baby?" Keisha stroked the damp hair away from Maria's face.

Maria began to rock back and forth. "I don't know. Why me? Why me?"

Only Fernandez could answer that question. Jack couldn't wait.

"SHANE and I will be back as soon as we can." Keisha reassured Maria. They had seemed to bond.

Maria nodded.

"Why don't you get some rest?" Bliss suggested.

"I can't. I can't sleep."

"Why don't you at least lie down on the sofa." Jack patted the cushions.

Maria shuffled to the sofa, her movements like a woman three times her age. She settled in the corner against the arm.

"I want to nail that bastard," Keisha said fiercely.

"We have to wait until we have Maria's DNA confirmation." Jack caught his employee in a one armed hug. "And then we will."

"How long do we have to wait?"

"We should have the results tomorrow." Bliss was still beating herself up over the fact that she hadn't realized that Maria needed touch, affection. She would have preferred to go get Maria her new clothes, but she'd lost her once and couldn't take the chance that Maria would bolt again.

"You two need to get to the clothing store before it closes," Jack directed.

Keisha nodded her agreement. "We need anything else?"

They agreed to bring back food for everyone.

"See you soon." Shane's deep voice echoed from the doorway. He held his arm across the doorway, and surveyed the parking lot and surrounding woods before he let Keisha exit.

"Seriously, dude?" Keisha tossed her curls. "I was in the damn Navy."

"Can't help it." Shane shrugged. "Don't care if you like it or not."

They continued bickering as the door swung shut.

"You okay?" Jack asked Bliss.

Apparently he'd noticed that she was upset about her lack of emotional attention to Maria.

Maria, who had fallen into a light doze. Bliss was thankful that she trusted them enough to fall asleep in their presence.

She gestured to the small kitchenette bar. "So, we've got Maria, we'll have the DNA results. I wish we had some way to tie him to the house."

Jack eyed her for another moment before he accepted that she didn't want to talk about it.

Jack took the seat next to her. His heat warmed the air and the scent of Jack surrounded her in a haze of comfort.

"We need a way to pressure him that will be so in his face that we break him."

"Something really public." Bliss set her computer on the kitchenette counter and booted it up so she could look on Fernandez's website for his appearance schedule. "We know he is here locally. Let's find out where he'll be tomorrow."

Jack grinned. "Hey, I have a friend who reports the local news. I bet I could get Charity to ask some pointed questions."

Bliss's curiosity rose as she wondered how close a friend Charity was. But before she could ask, there was a pounding at the door.

Jack strode toward the entrance to their room. "They must have forgotten something."

"Check the security peephole first."

Maria sat up groggily and rubbed at her eyes.

Jack shot her a look then pulled the tail of his t-shirt from his waist and put his hand around the grip of his weapon.

A strange uneasiness seized Bliss. "I don't have a good feeling about this."

Jack peered through the peephole. "No one there."

"Jack, get away from the door." Bliss's voice never rose but the panic was evident. "Maria, take cover."

She couldn't stop the sheer terror bubbling through her. Something was really wrong. She groped in her messenger bag for her weapon.

Suddenly the door splintered around the doorknob. Jack

pulled Maria to her feet and then yanked her down behind the sofa. "Stay down," he murmured fiercely. The sharp retort of silenced rounds as they punctured the flimsy wood were the only sounds in the room besides Bliss's frantic breath.

Bliss took cover behind the breakfast bar counter and peered around the side so she could see the doorway. Her heart bulleted in her chest. If Jack had still been standing in front of the door, he'd be full of holes right now.

Jack leveled his weapon at the doorway. "Get in the bedroom," he ordered them both.

Blood trickled down his temple. The sight paralyzed Bliss for a minute. "Were you hit?"

"No. I'm fine." Jack ignored the blood dripping onto his collar. He must have been hurt by flying wood slivers.

Two men burst through the door, their hands wrapped around their weapons. Bliss had seconds to process. Two men. Average height. One dark skinned, one lighter. Both wearing tan ski masks so their faces were not visible. But their appearances were ragged and desperate as if they'd been sleeping in their clothes.

After the initial barrage of bullets, the silence was deafening.

"No one move." One of the men ordered, his voice was gruff and uneven with a hint of an accent.

Maria whimpered at the sound of his voice.

Shit. They must be the men who kidnapped her and kept her prisoner for all those years.

"How'd you find us?" Jack asked.

"Who the fuck cares?" the dark skinned one said. His gun was pointed at Bliss. "Give us the girl and we'll let you go."

Girl? They couldn't possibly be talking about Maria?

The bigger, lighter skinned man held his weapon pointed at Jack and Maria. His arm was trembling.

This was a clusterfuck waiting to happen. Both the men were unsteady and close to complete meltdown.

Bliss stared at them, stared at the men responsible for Maria's suffering. Responsible for her years of captivity. Her fear. And all the rage that Bliss had suppressed for years jetted to the surface in a burst of adrenaline.

Bliss quit cowering behind the breakfast bar and stood tall. "Leave her alone."

"Jesus, Bliss." Jack snarled, "Get down."

"Forget about her, *chica*." The smaller one's hand trembled. "Save yourself."

All the years of suppressing her longing for her sister, her father, hoping for her family to be whole again, the hurt, the disillusionment when the marshals had decided to keep them separated forever. Every single attempt to find them, every single denial of her request to see them, rose up in a fireball of rage. "I will not let you hurt her anymore."

Jack shoved Maria to the floor and trying to draw both men's attention, shouted, "Get down."

The shout was the distraction they needed. Both men took their attention from their targets briefly. Bliss's heart shot to her throat. Dammit Jack.

"Shoulders." She commanded Jack and hoped he got her meaning.

Bliss practiced weekly at the Adams-Larsen indoor range. Their shots rang out simultaneously. The percussive blast was deafening in the small hotel suite.

Bliss's shot hit her target in the shoulder joint. He reflexively pulled his trigger but the shot went wide and hit the refrigerator.

"Bliss, get down, dammit."

Jack had hit his guy in the hand. He'd dropped the weapon and fortunately the gun didn't go off. Both the kidnappers dropped to the floor and howled.

Jack gave his gun to Maria. "Only shoot if you have to.

Jack pulled plastic zip ties from Shane's duffel. Bliss got up to help and he practically took her head off. "Stay behind the counter and cover me. Shoot them again if they make any move to get up.

Jack quickly restrained their arms behind their backs. And then Bliss was on the phone with Garrett. "We need medics."

After Jack got the ties on their feet, he ripped the mask from the first man's head. Maria stood tall and nodded. Bliss would never forget the look on her face. Pure satisfaction. "He's the one who raped Sofia."

Quickly Jack ripped off the other mask and Maria nodded again. "That's them."

Jack pulled identification from their pockets and flipped open the first man's wallet. As he took in their names, a feral satisfaction spread through him.

They had Fernandez now.

CHAPTER 11

The confrontation was set.

The men who'd broken into the hotel room were Fernandez's brothers. They had been on their way to make sure the house went up and saw Shane's car leaving the two lane road. So they had followed them back to their hotel and waited until Shane and Keisha left, believing they could scare Jack and Bliss into giving up Maria.

The men had no prior arrests or illegal activity on their records. They'd been model citizens which explained how they had managed to keep Maria a secret all those years. But when they'd been confronted with their complicity in kidnapping the girls and holding Maria prisoner, they had rolled over on Fernandez. He'd managed to hold Sofia's death over them for years.

Once they realized that Maria was communicating with the U.S. Marshals, they knew they were screwed. The marshals had managed to hold them overnight without the requisite phone calls, so Fernandez had no idea that he was going down.

Keisha had taken perfect care of Maria when they'd returned to the hotel.

Jack still wasn't sure he'd recovered from the danger to Bliss. At random times his heart would start to beat frantically and his blood pressure would rise. He'd seen the edge of fury in her eyes when she'd gone after the Fernandez brothers. She'd scared the hell out of him.

But the case was almost over.

The U.S. Marshals were here. Jess was on the roof of the building across the street with a camera rather than her sniper rifle.

It felt as if the entire world had gone crazy. Riley, who apparently had been out of communication for several days, was home from the Philippines and had a thing with Di Lundberg. Never in a million years would he have seen that coming. Con and Ava were together. Jess and Colin. Everyone had paired off and it felt unbelievably weird.

Riley, Connor, Colin, and Shane were going to be Maria's human wall. Ava and Keisha were on hand to rally around Maria.

Jack had decided to let Ava and Maria confront Fernandez.

Bliss was tucked away in the back of the room. She'd found the perfect vantage point to watch Fernandez get taken down. Adams-Larsen couldn't reveal their role in the care and protection of Maria so she was well out of the limelight.

Fernandez had a town hall meeting today at the VFW specifically for the Farm Workers Association. Jack couldn't have scripted this confrontation better if he'd tried.

Fernandez was dressed in Average José casual: Levi's, a plaid flannel shirt, and a pair of scuffed cowboy boots. But he still had the thousand dollar buffed and shined look beneath the Wal-Mart attire.

"Scumbag," Bliss muttered.

Jack had chosen to stay in the background with Bliss. She'd been all business, and since they'd found Maria yesterday, they'd had no time alone. Jack had coordinated with his brothers and sister while Bliss had worked with the U.S. Marshals to make sure this all went to plan.

The old hall was packed to the rafters with Fernandez's adoring public.

This was nothing more than a glorified photo op for Fernandez. Luckily it was a slow news day everywhere else because Jack was pretty sure this surprise was going to catapult Charity into a national figure by tonight. When Jack had approached her about the scoop, she'd initially been skeptical but once he showed her the evidence, she'd jumped at the chance to 'interview' Fernandez.

Jack had gone to several charity events with Charity but she was hung up on her ex, so nothing ever developed, which Jack now thought was ironic. Bliss had seemed to pick up on the fact that they were a little more than friends, which was one more hurdle to overcome once he finally got her alone.

Fernandez had a wide smile on his face while he waited for Charity to conduct her interview. She reapplied her lip gloss, fluffed her hair, and ran her tongue around her teeth, looking harmless and a little bit flighty. But beneath the beauty queen exterior was a shark waiting to attack.

Jack couldn't wait for Fernandez's smarmy smile to disappear.

Fernandez's expression was a practiced benevolence, as the print reporters snapped pictures. Then totally hot

Charity, with her long blonde hair, sparkling blue eyes, and Southern California tan, began her interview.

Her ocean blue eyes sharpened as she pandered to his ego, mentioning all of his former accomplishments. "And how are you feeling about the upcoming Senate confirmation vote?"

"I am hopeful that the Senate will agree that as a champion of a sector of the population that is usually ignored I will have a unique and positive impact on the future of employment for all the people. And especially the people who have supported me over the last eight years."

The crowd cheered. Whistles and catcalls echoed in the packed house.

Fernandez had perfected the politician's wave and raised both arms to encourage the crowd to get louder.

Once the noise died down Charity tilted her head, letting her blond hair fall over one shoulder in a flirty sway, then went in for the kill. "What about the accusations that you were involved in the abduction of the four girls? The tragedy that launched your career?"

The crowd hushed.

"Now, Charity," Fernandez sat back on the metal stool and placed his palms flat on his knees and leaned toward the crowd, all earnest, his brows crinkled in 'concern'. "Sadly, mental illness is shoved under the rug in our country. I would like to propose that we amend the laws so that people with these illnesses are not stigmatized but can get the help they need. Ava Sanchez, the girl who made those accusations, has...problems."

"Oh, I wasn't talking about Ava." Charity brought the microphone closer to her mouth, and paused for dramatic effect. That was the signal for Maria to start making her way across the stage.

Bliss grabbed his hand and squeezed tight. "This is it," she whispered.

Maria stepped out from behind the curtains on the stage, surrounded by all four large men, and holding tightly to Ava and Keisha's hands.

The crowd murmured, the noise growing louder with each second. Maria was still behind Fernandez but he'd taken note of the shift in the crowd's demeanor and was fidgeting on the utilitarian stool.

"I was talking about Maria Torres," Charity said, dropping the bomb.

Maria stepped into Fernandez's view.

Charity turned and asked Maria, "Who was responsible for your abduction and imprisonment?"

Maria was shaking but Keisha whispered encouragement in her ear. Maria lifted her arm and pointed straight at Fernandez.

Fernandez blanched as Charity shoved the microphone back into his swarthy face. "I don't know who this woman is but I assure you—"

Charity interrupted his denial. "DNA tests have already confirmed that this is Maria Torres who was abducted a little over eight years ago."

The entire crowd went completely silent. "Then it's a miracle." Fernandez lifted his gaze toward heaven, his smile shaky and sweat beaded on his upper lip, his hand trembled as he reached out toward Maria. "Praise Jesus."

But before he could get anywhere near her, Shane blocked his arm.

Bliss's nails dug into Jack's palm and her arm curled around his.

The marshals came from the other side of the stage.

"José Fernandez, you are under arrest for the abduction and false imprisonment of Maria Torres."

"Oh come now." Fernandez tried to bluster his way out of the situation. "You're taking the word of this...woman? She could have been anywhere. She could have run away."

Charity shook her head. "But she claims that you were instrumental—"

"I didn't have anything to do with keeping her in that basement," he blurted out desperately.

"We've fucking got him." Bliss squealed and threw her arms around Jack.

Jack wrapped his arms around her waist and pulled her into the curve of his arms, savoring her uninhibited glee. This was the closest she'd been to him in a day and a half.

A single tear leaked from the corner of her honey-colored eyes and trailed over her cheek. Jack cupped her face in his palms and brushed the tear away with his thumb. "You did it."

His gaze cut to the stage where the marshals were leading Fernandez away in handcuffs. Ava was hugging Maria, tears streaming down both their faces. They needed to get them out of here because the crowd was growing unruly. And Charity had taken the opportunity to try to get a more in-depth interview from Maria.

But Jack was struck with the realization that he had a chance to fix everything.

"My work here is done," Bliss quipped.

There were still a lot of details to get clear but there was one thing that Jack could do to make sure that he got the chance. "Stay for Thanksgiving."

"What?"

What he wanted to say was stay forever. But that was crazy, and she'd likely hop a plane back to the East Coast before he could backpedal if he actually spoke the wish aloud.

"Stay for Thanksgiving." They could talk later about everything but right now he just wanted to get her to agree to stick around for a few more days.

"I don't—"

"Stay." Jack entreated, "Please."

They were gathered in Jack's office, every chair was overflowing. Jack's sister Jess was sitting on Colin's lap. Riley and Di were crushed together in the large leather chair kitty corner to the sofa. Connor stood behind Ava who sat in the chair across from the desk. Marshal Garrett, Keisha and Maria were on the opposite sofa. Jack was perched on the edge of his desk. And Bliss was in the other single chair, feeling alone and overwhelmed.

They'd just finished a post-mortem on what had gone right and what they needed to work on.

"We definitely need some alternate way to communicate that isn't public. And can't be bugged or hacked." This was from Connor. He shot Bliss a look. "Especially if you're going to be out of pocket more often."

Bliss blushed.

"I'm never leaving my office again." Jack scowled at his desk.

And everyone snickered.

Clearly Bliss was missing something. The past few hours

had been eye-opening. Jack was definitely in charge. And for some reason, it was totally hot.

"Okay, you perverts." Jack crossed his arms over his chest. "Good news, Fernandez's brothers have given the DOJ enough to indict Fernandez. And they admitted that they were the ones who tried to abduct Ava."

Connor curled his arm around the pretty assistant and she laid her head on his shoulder. He bussed a kiss on her curls. "I can't believe they managed to keep the original crime secret all these years."

"Family can be a powerful motivator," Marshal Garrett answered.

All four Stone siblings smiled in complete understanding. Their obvious closeness was beautiful, and Bliss ached for the loss of her sister and father.

"And since we have an eye witness." Marshal Garrett laid a gentle hand on Maria's shoulder. "It was in their best interests to cooperate."

Keisha grinned fiercely at Maria. Keisha had turned into a Mama Bear. She wouldn't let anyone get too close to Maria.

Tears spilled from Maria's deep, sorrowful brown eyes. "Thank you all," her voice rasped. She still wasn't used to speaking, and every word sounded like an effort to push through her vocal chords. "Will we ever find out what happened to my other friends?"

"Hopefully they'll give up their contact. And we can find out what happened to the other two girls. But," Jack paused. "They insist they only dealt with the trafficker once so it may be a dead end."

The other two girls had disappeared. Likely sold. For whatever reason, Fernandez had felt guilty about abducting Maria. He couldn't bring himself to let her be sold, he couldn't kill her, so he had secreted her away in that forgotten basement.

"Ava already has the plan in place to make *S.S.A.F.E.*, Security, Shelter, and Freedom for the Exploited, the next philanthropy that GHR supports. We'll see if they can help us figure out where to start looking for the girls," Jack said.

Ava held tight to Maria's hands.

"I want this guy to pay," Connor said fiercely.

"Con is still tracing the ownership of Banke of America," Jack said proudly.

"Now that I have a lead, I should have something in the next day or two." Con brushed a lock of hair from his blue eyes, his gaze on Ava and Maria. "Fuck me, but that's a beautiful sight."

Jess rested her back against Colin's chest and tilted her head to grin at him. "If he somehow gets out, I can always shoot him."

Colin lifted a pale brow and Jess laughed.

Riley only had eyes for the tall, blond-haired woman who sat next to him. Bliss was quiet as they finalized the rest of the details. Maria was going to live with Ava for now. Connor didn't look thrilled, until Ava leaned over and whispered something in his ear. And his expression changed at her shy smile.

With each revelation and interaction between Jack's siblings, Bliss's discomfort grew. The need to escape, flee, fizzed through her bloodstream. She didn't belong here. Jack had this whole family who clearly worshipped him. And loved him.

"We're done here." Jack abruptly closed the meeting.

But everyone continued to lounge around his office chatting among themselves.

"Everybody out." Jack waved his large blunt tipped

fingers in a shooing motion which seemed to be the prod that got people to leave. Keisha and Ava surrounded Maria keeping her cocooned as if to protect her from the world. Riley twirled Diana around and dipped her. Di flushed, but didn't stop him, a sweet smile curved her mouth. His smooth actions were a curious contrast to Jack's gruff manner.

Slowly, they filed out of his office. Each sibling shot Jack, then Bliss, a curious look. She gathered up her messenger bag and hefted it on to her shoulder.

"Not you," Jack growled at Bliss.

Bliss paused. She wanted to be done. She needed out of this office, out of California, and away from Jack. "I can have Jillian give you a call about the mission details."

"I could give a rat's ass about Jillian," Jack dismissed her offer.

"Smooth, Jack," Riley said as he closed the door to Jack's office.

"Shut up! I don't need to be you to get my own girl." Jack's face scrunched into a frown. He looked like a little kid who was denied his favorite treat.

His girl? Bliss's pulse thudded hard.

Jack turned away from the closed office door and took in the surprise on Bliss's face. He had finally figured out that if he was going to convince her to stay, he was going to have to share some things with her. Jack threaded his fingers through hers and tugged her over to the recently vacated sofas.

"I should probably go." She hunched her shoulders and tried without success to extricate her fingers from his.

"When I was fourteen my father left."

Bliss stopped trying to untangle their fingers. "Left, how?"

"He handed over the responsibility of my siblings and my...step mother, for want of a better word, and took off." He pulled her down to sit close beside him, their thighs pressed up against each other. Jack forced himself to ignore the heat from her body. As much as he wanted to just pull her into his arms and convince her with sex that she should stay, that wasn't going to cut it.

"Um, Jack?"

"For the next six years, I took care of everyone. It was —" He paused, swallowed. "So, fast forward to when I met you." He rubbed his index finger along her wrist and then over their laced fingers. "For the first time in my life, I was only responsible for me, and I kind of embraced the idea that I didn't have to watch out for everyone else."

"You really don't have to—"

"I really do." He lifted their twined fingers and pressed his mouth to her knuckles.

Bliss fell silent.

"I'm a protector," Jack said.

"I don't...." Bliss hesitated. "Where are you going with this?"

"I'm baring my soul here," Jack joked. "Pay attention."

But his heart was pounding and nerves roiled in his stomach. What if it was too late? What if she didn't care anymore?

But what if he didn't do this? He'd definitely lose her.

"When you." His throat got tight. Jack coughed. "Cut me loose. It was like I lost a piece of me. I had to go through with Basic but I was a fucking mess. You cut me off at the knees, Bliss."

She opened her mouth but he put a finger over her lips to stop her from speaking.

"Once I got out of the Navy, I knew what I needed to

do." His heart thudded in his chest. "My goal in creating the company was to find a safe place for all of my siblings and to keep us together. We're stronger together. And honestly, we were all drifting a bit."

He understood from the beginning that they were stronger together than they were apart. They each brought a skill and a unique perspective to the table and their family. Unfortunately his siblings didn't always get what he was trying to do. He was intuitive enough to understand that Jess still felt like an outsider and that Connor was still trying to prove himself. Riley he had never figured out. But he knew to the depths of his soul that Riley was the loyalty and heart of the Stone family. They just needed Jack to bring them all back together.

Jack took a breath.

"I figured out after a few months, that I needed them just as much as they needed me." He toyed with the top button of her plain white button up shirt.

"That's really beautiful Jack but I'm not sure what that has to do with me." Her face was impassive, her expression merely curious.

He was confessing things he'd never told another soul. In a roundabout way, he was trying to tell her that he needed her, just as much as he needed his siblings. But he was also terrified of how much he felt for her.

Objectively he watched as her heart beat hard in the hollow of her throat. The strength of the shimmy in her breasts as the organ pounded gave him hope. She wasn't as unaffected as she tried to appear.

"The company has exceed, maybe even surpassed, my vision when I came up with the idea."

Her smile was bittersweet as she brushed her thumb over his scarred eyebrow. "I'm happy for you, Jack."

Her honey eyes were glassy and she'd started trying to tug her hand away again.

"Yeah, but my vision was missing something really important." Jack flattened her fingers over his heart.

"I, I—" Bliss shot off the sofa. "I need to go."

"You need to stay," Jack countered and stood. "My vision was missing you, Bliss."

"That's crazy." Bliss tried to back away, but Jack wasn't letting her go this time. Her eyes were panicked, and her pulse fluttered, and her breath came in quick pants.

"When I hired Ava she made me remember what I'd forgotten. To seize each day. Not to take anything for granted. Because tomorrow it could all be gone."

"Great words to live by." Bliss was practically hyperventilating. "Got to go."

She beelined for the exit.

But Jack beat her to the door, and backed her up against the closed wood panel. "I'm not letting you go. Not again. I'm going to seize the day. I'm going to seize you."

Jack curved one palm against her cheek, wrapped the other arm around her waist, and pulled her flush against his body.

"Please don't shut me out again." Because that's what he'd realized after their conversation the other night. She'd been terrified of their intimacy.

Bliss dropped her forehead to his chest. Her breath puffed against his pecs. "I was only trying to protect myself," she whispered.

"You should have let me protect you. That's what I do," he whispered back.

And finally, she curled her arms around his waist and held him back.

Jack stood to his full height, twirled her around, and

started walking her backwards toward his desk and away from the exit. "God, I promise never to take this for granted."

"What?"

"You. Us. Finding you again." Jack knew it was sappy. Knew he was baring his soul so deep that he'd never survive if she walked away. But he knew, just knew, that if he did this, a greater reward awaited. "Promise me you'll always tell me what's in your heart."

Bliss put her hand over her chest, like a little kid and crossed her index finger in an x. "I promise. As long as you promise the same. So we don't repeat the mistakes of the past."

"I promise." His voice was deep, thick as gratitude overwhelmed him. "I love you."

"I love you too." Her honey eyes were warm and overflowing with that love.

The past was over. But their future was bright, happy, unlimited as long as they had each other.

And then he looked at where Bliss was standing, his body swelled with happiness and the lust he'd worked hard to suppress while he confessed he needed her.

"What are you thinking about right now?" Bliss dropped back to perch on his desk, a bright smile lit her face. A deep satisfaction brightened her honey eyes and made them sparkle.

Jack slid his arms around her shoulders and nudged his way between her thighs. A lightness filled his heart, a lightness that had been missing for thirteen years. "You're on my lucky desk." At least it was about to be *his* lucky desk. Why not? It had worked for his sister and brothers.

She laughed, the sound sweet music to his ears. "Why is it lucky?"

"Let me show you," he growled. And they both got lucky. Twice.

The entire family was gathered around Mom's massive dining room table. They only used it a few times a year but when the whole family was together Mom went all out. The giant mahogany table was covered with a deep gold tablecloth and laden with so much food it nearly sagged. In the middle was a blown glass turkey, candlesticks of every shape and size scattered down the center along with silk, fall-colored leaves and gourds and mini-pumpkins.

Riley and Di carried the huge turkey in on a giant ceramic platter. Together they set it down in front of Mom. Their tradition had always been to slice the turkey at the table. Riley had requested a full-on, load the table traditional, Thanksgiving dinner because Diana had never celebrated Thanksgiving. Jack could barely stand how unbelievably sweet that was, but he figured he'd tease Riley later in private, because he didn't want to embarrass Di. And honestly, he'd been a little on sweet side himself since he and Bliss had reunited.

"Look out, Mom's got the knife," Riley teased as he held

Di's chair for her. Jack watched his subtle caress along Di's graceful neck.

This year everything seemed brighter, more vibrant. The smashed orange sweet potatoes, the yellow grilled corn on the cob, the perfectly browned and crisped skin of the turkey, the deep burgundy of the cranberry sauce were great splashes of color on the table. But nothing was more vibrant or colorful than the woman beside him. Her dress was a simple shift with blocks of all the colors that graced the table.

Noise filled the room. Happy noise. They were all together for Thanksgiving. And this year there was so much to give thanks for, Jack thought, as he slowly looked at his brothers and sister and their newfound partners. What a wild and crazy month November had turned out to be.

Bliss slid her palm against his and clasped their hands together. He'd never been more thankful than right this moment. "What are you thinking about right now?"

God, he didn't think he'd ever take this for granted. Finding her again. They'd made a vow to always tell each other what was in their hearts. To not repeat the mistakes of the past.

But that didn't mean he couldn't have a little fun. A secret smile curved Jack's mouth as he leaned over to whisper in her ear, "What I'm going to do to you later."

Her honey eyes brightened with interest, and laughter. "I like it." She brought their clasped fists to her lips and kissed his knuckles, leaving behind a smudge of deep burgundy lipstick. "But that's *not* what you're thinking about."

Jack sobered and held her gaze. "I'm thinking about how thankful I am for you, for my family." Then he leaned in and kissed her, right there, in front of everyone.

"Jack and Bliss sitting in a tree," Jess taunted.

"K-I-SS-I-N-G," Connor finished then laughed. Ava giggled.

"I thought you didn't approve of public displays of affection, mate." Colin slung his arm around Jess's shoulders and his fingers toyed with her hair.

Jack hadn't imagined that they could all be together like this. Happy, laughing, content. Finally his father's legacy had led to something good. Something they could hold on to. Something they could cherish.

The doorbell rang, in a deep, three-toned chime.

Shelley looked up from carving the turkey. "I wonder who that could be."

There was only one person missing from today's family celebration and Jack guaranteed no one wanted him here. "I'll get it."

Jack pushed out of his chair and strode to the front door, ready to kick the old man to the curb if his father had dared to show up at their family celebration. Nothing was going to ruin this day.

But when he opened the door, a guy he'd never seen before stood on the gaily decorated porch. Pumpkins and hay bundles and bright happy mums were scattered over the limestone steps. But, not his father, thank God.

"Can I help you?"

The man held a Marine Barracks Cover in his hands, dressed in a service uniform, military posture stiff and uncomfortable. Jack noted other details peripherally. He had black hair sprinkled with a little gray, cheekbones that looked eerily familiar, and signature deep set hazel eyes.

"I'm looking for Jack Stone."

"You got him." But a weird, buzzing grew in his ears as he registered he was looking straight into the guy's eyes.

They were almost the same height, and their chest and shoulders were equally broad.

The guy blinked. His eyes widened. Then he straightened his back, shoulders as if ready to do battle.

"Jack, you're taking awfully long. Who is it?" Shelley teased as she came up beside him. Her face paled when she finally saw the man in the doorway.

"Be right there, Mom." Jack turned back to the guy, his suspicions growing by the second. "You aren't looking for me."

"No." The guy rubbed the edge of his hat with familiar looking blunt tipped fingers, and said, "I guess I'm looking for Jack Stone, Senior. My father."

THANK you for reading Jack and Bliss's story. I hope you enjoyed reading Still the One as much as I enjoyed writing it. If you did enjoy this novella, below are a few ways you can help a writer out!!

Good: Lend the book to a friend

Better: Recommend the book to your friends

Best: Leave a review at Amazon, BN, Goodreads, Kobo, iBooks and Google Play…basically any place they sell or review eBooks. Every review helps my work get out to other readers and I cannot even express how much it means to me when you let people know you liked my work. Readers have so many choices nowadays and limited dollars to spend. It can be difficult to take a chance on a new author even if the premise sounds appealing. By reviewing books, you give other readers insight into the story world and help them make informed purchases.

· · ·

THANK YOU, thank you, thank you for your support!!

P.S. Would you like to know when my next book is available? You can sign up for Lisa's Confidants and never miss a new release

EXCERPT OF STONE COLD HEART

Family Stone #1 Jess

In the early evening dusk, Jess Stone lay on her stomach in the twenty foot high rubble of a demolished church, underneath a black and gray city-scape tarp intended to camouflage her position. A sharp-edged chunk of debris dug into her lower rib cage, the scope of the Remington M24 cool and familiar against her face.

Her standard uniform of jeans, running shoes, and plain black t-shirt rendered her just another anonymous and transient relief worker...which she was actually. A black baseball cap hid her distinctive multi-hued blonde hair. The paper mask kept out the contaminated dust from the destroyed buildings but did little to stem the overwhelming stench of decaying bodies.

Tanks rumbled through the destroyed coastal town, their public address system blasting warnings for citizens to stay in their homes, curfew was in effect. The threat was a joke. Ninety percent of the people in the town didn't have homes left. Those who did were terrified to go back inside. In the fetid, humidity choked air, the tent cities erected in the parks and on the beach were seething masses of the injured and shock struck.

The substandard construction in the small country had never been enough to withstand the angry might of Mother Nature. Buildings had toppled like a stack of Tinkertoys, and left crumbling cement walls with twisted rebar poking out of the jagged ruins like a skeletal hand.

Trapped in the concrete pieces that littered the ground, the heat from the tropical day seared through her thin sturdy clothing. The stank of the raw sewage that ran in rivulets through the streets overpowered the salt-laden breeze off the ocean. People, covered with the grit of pulverized buildings and humans, shuffled along with blank vacant stares. Two weeks after the quake, still in shock, their lives decimated first by nature and then kicked and beaten by the ineffectiveness of a flawed relief system. Hundreds of humanitarian agencies had descended on the population duplicating efforts and yet completely missing the need in other areas. The government was ostensibly trying to coordinate the effort, however the mass chaos was undeniable.

Through the Leupold Ultra M3 fixed power sight, she tracked the movements of Henri LeRoy, leader of this tiny island nation, violator of human rights and dignity, and all around poor excuse for a human being.

Sickness roiled in her stomach. The power bar she'd eaten for breakfast threatened to add to the rubble pile as she tried to figure out how in the hell she'd ended up here. Back behind a sniper rifle with the power over life and death trembling in the muscles of her right trigger finger.

Dammit. When she'd decided to take control of her life and quit the FBI, she hadn't wanted to do this anymore.

She'd wanted to be a simple relief worker. She'd wanted to connect with her family, brothers and mother.

But that bitch, fate, had slapped her upside the head and now here she was, where she'd sworn she never wanted to be again. Looking through the scope of a high-powered rifle, with a crystal clear head shot and a murky sense of right and wrong.

With little fanfare, she could blast LeRoy's brain matter all over the silk-covered walls and the antique Louis the XIV scrolled chairs in the receiving room of his ridiculously elegant weekend mansion which, since built properly, had sustained minimal damage. Her muscles twitched with the knowledge and acceptance that with one slow slide of her finger, the despotic, amoral leader would be history.

Jess didn't want to kill him, didn't want to be directly responsible for another death. She didn't want this choice. She'd given up this kind of life. She'd left the FBI after a series of high stress cases to get away from the doubt and guilt that had crippled her. To make her own decisions about right and wrong rather than carry out the commands of her bosses.

But if Henri LeRoy lived, chances were astronomical that many other citizens would die.

And yeah, she'd probably been manipulated into this. Actually no probably about it. Assassination had not been listed as one of her duties when she'd joined Global Humanitarian Relief. Damn her brother anyway.

But now all she could do was lay here in the desecrated remains of the former church and hope that her special skill set wouldn't be needed.

Fortunately, she was secondary backup.

And unless several things went horribly wrong, she would break down her weapon, get back to the relief aid encampment, back to actually helping people, and be out of here without ever firing her rifle.

Then she could hand out seed packets to her heart's content and figure out what she was going to do next. If she'd stay with GHR and her brothers, or go. First, she had to get through the next two hours.

But if something did go wrong...she prayed that if she was called upon, she could make the right decision. Make the shot. Cold zero.

Blowback (blo′ bak) *n.* A deadly, unintended consequence of a covert operation.

Eerie blue light penetrated my consciousness first. The regulated thump-thump of tires pounded in my head, echoing with fierce resonance.

Where the hell was I? Why did I feel like this? I kept my eyes closed, knowing pretense was paramount to my survival. Wherever I was, it wasn't normal.

Ha. My life would never be normal.

I tracked back to my last memory. I'd hooked up with a guy. Had relatively indiscriminate sex with him.

I inhaled shallowly, carefully, not wanting to give away anything. I still smelled like sex. Really great sex.

I wanted to smile but kept my expression lax.

I'd longed to stay in that bed. Sleep with him. Just sleep with the comforting warmth of another human being. The ache had been so intense that as soon as he dozed off--I left.

That was my last memory.

"You can stop pretending."

I continued to fake sleep. I didn't know that male voice.

It was bland, not angry, but with a slight smirk, as if he knew something I didn't.

"You should be awake by now. We calibrate our doses very carefully."

That statement raised so many questions, I decided to comply with his unspoken request and let my eyes drift open. I calculated we were moving at a speed of about thirty miles per hour. Suburban, blacked out windows, bulletproof glass. The blue light came from the interior dome in the big SUV.

"The light is to protect your eyes. The drug affects your pupil's ability to dilate and contract."

What drug? I kept silent.

"Not very curious, are you?"

My last conscious memory was from the motel off of 295 near Alexandria around nine in the evening. It was pitch dark out now, so I'd been out for a while.

Lucas. Could the guy have been a plant? Possible. Since he was my last clear memory, it made sense.

I sifted through the spaghetti of my brain. For the past two days, I'd been undercover, shadowing Staci Grant's life. Last night, I'd encountered Lucas Goodman, who'd been looking for Staci and thought he'd found her when he found me. The sexual heat between us had been instantaneous and mutual. A few sweaty hours later, I'd left, confident my movements as Staci had been tracked. My cover had been working.

They'd kidnapped Staci.

Excellent.

I was right where I needed to be.

Now I needed answers. My task was to discover why CIA, DIA, and NSA agents were being kidnapped, the method of interrogation, and who was doing the

kidnapping. The answers would be coming. I just had to
be ready.

I settled into the backseat of the car to wait, taking in
details. Mistake number one. They hadn't taken my ring, so
the satellite audio transmitter should work. I twisted the
unusual ring with my thumb and pressed the citrine stone
twice. I was now sending voice-activated recordings back to
Carson.

Mistake number two. They'd cuffed my hands, in front,
but left my legs unshackled.

They'd taken my government firearm but missed the
knife in the sheath at my waist. Mistake number three.
Always, always check everywhere for hidden weapons.

Although my mind was the most powerful weapon
I had.

My watch was gone and my government-issue GPS with
it. Slouching to the side, I got a better view of the dashboard
panel. My kidnapper had conveniently supplied me with
another GPS system, live and tracking.

Coordinates. Latitude–47. Longitude–122. I was in the
Pacific Northwest. I looked out the misted window to see a
reflection of the Space Needle and pinpointed my location
as Seattle. I was a long way from Virginia.

I returned my gaze to the kidnapper. Subject was male,
small head, blond hair gelled into little spikes, crescent-
shaped birthmark below his right ear.

The car rolled to a stop. The rocking intensified my
queasy stomach. I ignored it.

"We're here."

Here was a warehouse near the water. The guy wasn't
rough but the sudden motion as he lugged me out of the
SUV caused my stomach to roil.

I breathed in the cold, damp air through my nose, trying

to quell the nausea. As he led me toward a semi-truck trailer, I noted the parking lot was empty except for one other truck and a car, too far away and too dark to make out details. The warehouse, constructed with long cinder block walls interrupted by doors at twenty foot intervals, was to my left and behind me.

The trailer was modified from a regular shipping container, doors locked up tight in the back, with another entrance on the side. It looked as if the stairs were all one solid block which could fold up into the interior of the trailer.

The recessed entrance looked exactly like an old-fashioned front door complete with screen door. A porch light flicked on. The screen door wheezed open as a dark-haired woman in a white coat stepped out onto the platform.

The light behind her filled the doorway with shadows. I couldn't make out her features but I caught a furtive movement, the light illuminating her hand as she tucked a syringe into her pocket.

"Thank you. You can go now." She nodded regally to the man holding me. Her melodic voice held a hint of Asia, probably second-generation American.

He promptly let go of my arm and walked away. They must believe that the plastic restraint cuffs would be a big deterrent to resistance. The click of his heels echoed in the silence as she stared at me, her hands clasped tightly in front of her, so tightly her knuckles showed white.

There was something in her stance--tension, stress? I eased back a step.

"Welcome." She put a hand on the railing and took a step down. Then she hesitated and glanced back at the open doorway. "We won't hurt you."

I thought about the syringe in her pocket. *No thank you.*

I'd had drug resistance training but honestly I didn't want to put it to the test. At least, not yet. Although if that scenario became unavoidable and they pumped me full of drugs, the transmitter in my ring guaranteed I would get the information Carson and the NSA needed.

All of the kidnapped agents had an unidentified drug in their bloodstream and unknown consequences from those drugs. We had no idea what national secrets they'd given away or what kind of long-term effects were possible from the drug cocktail most likely in that syringe. My job was to get myself kidnapped, acquire the drugs, identify the perpetrators, and get out before they could accomplish their objective.

I wobbled as if unsteady on my feet and eased back two steps, assessing my position.

As the Suburban left, the beam from the head lamps shone on her. The shape of her face and the tilt of her eyes marked her as Chinese. Lines of strain curled around her mouth, the expression was supposed to be a smile but came off as more of a grimace. "Come with me."

I don't think so.

I'd expected the kidnapping, the intel suggested that Staci Grant would be next. I'd planned to resist at first. I didn't want to make it too easy for them to subdue me. Carson was supposed to have a team on standby waiting to capture the kidnappers after I completed my objectives. But since we hadn't planned for a cross country abduction—all of the other kidnappings had been local and accomplished within a matter of several hours—it would most likely take a little time before the extraction team got here.

If they got here.

I pivoted and ran for the warehouse door nearest me. Her footsteps rang on the metal steps as she followed.

"She's getting away." A man's shout, older, deeper, slightly frantic, registered as I reached the door. Two against one. More difficult, but not impossible. Woman, older man. Until I saw his physique, I couldn't judge who was more dangerous.

"I've got it," the woman replied and sprinted toward me.

I yanked on the handle, flung the door open, and slid inside. The heavy metal swung shut with an ominous clang.

Obviously, the drugs were making me melodramatic.

The warehouse was dimly lit. Industrial metal lights hung from the ceiling, their muted pink glow making the surroundings blurry. Metal shelving separated the concrete floor into long, wide aisles. Three tiers of jumbo shelves housed wooden pallets of goods. I stood at the end of one aisle.

I hustled over two aisles, pulling the knife from the sheath at my waist as I went. The restraint cuffs at my wrists took a few swipes before slicing clean through.

I grabbed some small ceramic rice bowls and shoved them into my jacket pockets. Mistake number four. They'd let me keep my jacket.

The door banged open.

"Don't let her escape." I could hear the man huffing, and a rhythmic thumping noise as they pursued.

"She won't escape," the woman replied grimly from somewhere behind me.

I stalked down the industrial cement aisle, my footsteps silent. Glancing around, I searched for another way out.

"Please don't try to escape, Agent Hunt." The man's plea had a desperate edge to it.

My legs faltered. I wanted to stop, stand rooted to the floor. Only training kept me moving.

He'd spoken my real name. My *real* name, not the cover I was using for this assignment. So who did they really want?

Me, Jamie Hunt, NSA agent? Or Staci Grant, CIA officer?

ACKNOWLEDGMENTS

Huge thanks to my BIL Ed for giving the Stone Family the proper private jet! I promise that Jack never complains about how much it costs to insure it.

Thank you to LJ at Mayhem Cover Creations for the beautiful cover!!

And once again, major, major thanks to Adrienne Bell and LGC Smith for everything under the sun.

<u>Cold as Stone (John, Family Stone #7)</u>

<u>Family Stone Box Set (Stone Cold Heart, Carved in Stone, Heart of Stone, Still the One, & Jar of Hearts)</u>

<u>The Nostradamus Prophecies</u>

<u>View To A Kill #1</u>

Never Say Never #2

<u>ALIAS</u>

Stalked (ALIAS #1)

Hunted (ALIAS #2)

Vanished (ALIAS #3)

Deceived (ALIAS #4)

<u>Billionaire Breakfast Club</u>

His Semi-Charmed Life (Camp Firefly Falls #11 and Billionaire Breakfast Club #0)

Everything He Wants (Billionaire Breakfast Club #1 The Jock)

Queen of His Daydreams (Camp Firefly Falls #23 and Billionaire Breakfast Club #1.5)

Stone Cold Heart:

Jess Stone, former FBI sniper, always felt like the kid who looks in the candy store window but could never afford to go in. But on a humanitarian mission to aid an earthquake ravaged country, finally she finds a place where she fits, in Colin Davies' arms, and working for Global Humanitarian Relief, her big brother's company. But can the former SAS thaw Jess's stone cold heart?

Carved in Stone:

Connor Stone has always been odd man out in his family. Not the oldest, not the most charming, he'd had a lock on the youngest until another half-sibling came to live with them, so he raised hell in his youth. Con knows now the only way to redeem himself is with deeds, not words and sets out to prove once and for all he is worthy of the Stone family. When his older brother asks him to take care of business, Con finally will have redemption he craves. Except when Ava Sanchez, his brother's assistant, is threatened, he must choose between saving the girl or protecting his family. Will his choice bring him love or break his heart?

Heart of Stone:

Riley Stone is the handsome brother, the charming one. Everyone who meets him compares him to his father, which in his mind is not a compliment. But he's never met a woman he couldn't charm, until he meets Di, an acerbic, smart-mouthed, passionate activist who has no time for him or his charm. On the run, in the midst of danger, the blistering passion they share explodes. Can these two opposites find common ground, or will Di smash Riley's stone heart?

Still the One:

Jack Stone, former Navy SEAL, and oldest Stone sibling is determined to keep his family strong. Family is everything. So he starts Global Humanitarian Relief and Stone Consulting to do some good and keep his family together. But when he has to team up with his old flame, Bliss, on a missing persons case, an evil threatens him, his family and the one woman he could never forget and doesn't want to let go. Can these two former lovers put aside past hurts and heal their hearts?

USA Today Bestselling Author Lisa Hughey started writing romance in the fourth grade. That particular story involved a prince and an engagement. Now, she writes about strong heroines who are perfectly capable of rescuing themselves and the heroes who love both their strength and their vulnerability. She pens romances of all types—suspense, paranormal, and contemporary—but at their heart, all her books celebrate the power of love.

She lives in Cape Ann Massachusetts with her fabulously supportive husband, two out of three awesome mostly-grown kids, and one somewhat grumpy cat.

Beach walks, hiking, and traveling are her favorite ways to pass the time when she isn't plotting new ways to get her characters to fall in love.

Lisa loves to hear from readers and has tons of places you can connect with her. It's a wonder she gets any writing done at all....

Sign Up for Lisa's Confidants
Visit Lisa on the Web

Follow Lisa's Boards on Pinterest
Follow Lisa on Instagram
Email Lisa
Be Lisa's Friend on Goodreads
Like Lisa on Facebook at Lisa Hughey: My Books